W9-BDV-769

THE WORD FOR
YES

ALSO BY CLAIRE NEEDELL

Nothing Real, Volumes 1–3
Available as ebooks only

THE WORD FOR
YES

CLAIRE NEEDELL

HARPER TEEN
An Imprint of HarperCollinsPublishers

HarperTeen is an imprint of HarperCollins Publishers.

The Word for Yes
Copyright © 2016 by Claire Needell
All rights reserved. Printed in the United States of America.
No part of this book may be used or reproduced in any manner whatsoever without
written permission except in the case of brief quotations embodied in critical articles
and reviews. For information address HarperCollins Children's Books, a division of
HarperCollins Publishers, 195 Broadway, New York, NY 10007.
www.epicreads.com

Library of Congress Control Number: 2015940712
ISBN 978-0-06-236049-6 (trade bdg.)

Typography by Kate Engbring
16 17 18 19 20 CG/RRDH 10 9 8 7 6 5 4 3 2 1

First Edition

To Edith, Emily, and Jane

THE WORD FOR
YES

1

Alone at the breakfast table, Melanie still wore her pajamas—pink shorts and a matching tank with white flowers; her hair was pulled off her face by a dark purple headband. Her face shone from vigorous morning scrubbing. Her feet were bare, and she was chilly in the air-conditioned apartment, but too lazy to get her sweater or slippers from the bedroom she shared for twenty-four more hours with her sister, Erika. Melanie was supposed to get up early to help Dad pack his moving boxes, but she hadn't set her alarm. It was late, she knew that, but what was summer vacation for, if not sleeping in? At any rate, her sisters weren't doing much work either, from what Melanie could see, and Dad was not even around.

Erika, who was sixteen and a year ahead of Melanie at Rose Dyer High School, lay curled up on the couch in the adjacent living room reading a large book with a diagram of something that looked like an atom or a cell on the cover. The Russells lived in a three-bedroom apartment in Battery Park City, overlooking the Hudson River. It was a largish apartment for the neighborhood, but still felt cramped to Melanie, who often wished they could afford a townhouse, or a duplex, someplace with stairs. She thought if they had stairs she could get along better with Erika, who was nearly always in her way, and was generally too large for the apartment. Melanie, like her oldest sister, Jan, was petite, while Erika was tall, and given to taking up the entire couch, so no one else could sit there. Even if Erika had a more normal personality, Melanie thought she might hate her simply for her size. Big people annoyed Melanie. Even though Erika was skinny as a rail, her arms and legs were rangy, and she took up far more space than Melanie did in the small room they had been forced to live in together for the last fifteen years, simply because neither of them had the good sense, as Jan had, to be born first.

Jan, who was leaving for college the next day (and surrendering her room to Erika!), stood near the table drinking coffee. Jan was dressed in cobalt-blue shorts and a white peasant blouse. She didn't look dressed to help anyone pack boxes, but more like she was off to get brunch with her boyfriend, Adam. Anyway, that's what Melanie would be doing if she were leaving town tomorrow. Melanie, exhausted, lay her head down on the table. She had been up until two, reading a novel from the summer homework list, and she still had an entire nonfiction book about climate change to read and write about in the next week. Summer homework was a stupid waste of time. "I don't know why

I got up. Dad's not even packing. What time is it?" Melanie asked.

"It's nine thirty," her mother answered. Julia Russell had just come out of her bedroom and was dressed for a meeting, although Melanie hadn't remembered her mother mentioning that she'd be leaving Melanie and her sisters to deal with Dad's move. It was classic. Mom had some business meeting on the day Dad planned to move out. It was better than her mother causing a major scene, Melanie figured, but in a way it was just as dramatic. Her mother was definitely trying to prove something, but what, Melanie couldn't say—that she wasn't going to help Dad with anything ever again? That he had to run his own life from now on? Or that she didn't need him? She was already too busy to hang around on his last day ever as her husband.

Julia Russell was a fashion writer and worked mostly from home, unless she had a meeting, and then she was usually dressed as she was now—pencil skirt, sleeveless blouse, strappy sandals, hair swooped into a low, messy bun. Julia was stylish and young-looking, though she had gray around her temples that she refused to color. She said it made her look less desperate than the women her age who insisted on being blond, "like a band of aging sorority girls."

"Dad's packing in there," Mom said, gesturing toward the bedroom, as she cleared a crumb-filled plate from the table. She said these words casually, as if he were going on an overnight trip and not moving everything he owned to a storage locker in Bushwick.

Jan caught Melanie's eye across the table, frowned, and

shook her head, annoyed. Jan, unlike Melanie, wasn't stuck forever in Battery Park to deal with her parents' separation. Not that their parents saw it as anything anyone else had to cope with. They acted like the whole thing would barely be noticed, as though Dad had always just been visiting, as though his long trips overseas on previous book projects had been rehearsals for this inevitable day when he'd leave for good. For a moment, a heavy silence hung over them, until it was broken by Erika, who leaped up suddenly from her place on the couch.

"Darn it," Erika exclaimed. "Friggenhoffer!" Erika had accidentally kicked a mug of hot tea from the side table, spilling its contents onto the new off-white area rug. But Erika couldn't swear like a normal person. She had to use corny words that made her sound like a total imbecile. Erika was a walking mishap. Why her mother bothered to buy anything nice while Erika lived there, Melanie did not know.

"Oh, for God's sake," her mother said, exasperated. Erika ran for the kitchen, practically hyperventilating.

"Sorry, Mom!" she said, dashing back and forth with rolls of paper towels and a bottle of stain remover. Erika was frantically blotting at the spot, spraying it with the stinking chemical cleaner, getting hysterical as the tea stain refused to be scrubbed away. Sympathetic, Jan picked up the empty teacup, patting Erika on the back as Erika tearfully dabbed at the carpet. "Oh, God, I ruined it," Erika said. "That was so stupid, an infinitude of stupid! Your new rug, Mom!" Erika kneeled on the carpet, vigorously rubbing the stain. "Ugh. It'll never be perfect."

"Okay, Erika, it's not that big a deal," Julia said evenly. "That's why I got it. Shows almost nothing." Mom had bought the rug the week before, along with a new deep red armchair, a set of velvet-trimmed pillows, and a bulbous, modern-looking lamp. Melanie could tell her mother was annoyed about the stain, but she was tiptoeing around Erika. If it had been Melanie who'd spilled something, it would be another story. Everyone always assumed the worst about Melanie.

It was odd that Mom was redecorating before Dad even moved out. Dad was leaving the country for six months to research a book about a Hong Kong real estate tycoon. At first, that was the only reason he was leaving, to work on his book. But then Mom put her foot down, insisting that he either stop with his excuses for spending half the year away, or move out permanently so she could have a "real life." Melanie had heard her mother use that phrase a dozen times, each time accusing Dad of being unwilling to "live a real life together." It gave her a chill each time she heard her say it. Did she mean the summers they spent in that spider-infested cabin in Maine hadn't been real? Their dinners out in Chinatown, all the family trips to Puerto Rico and Mexico, the time they went to Paris and she bought blue suede boots and tried frogs' legs, which tasted like fishy chicken? None of that had been real for her mother? That there was something false about her childhood gave Melanie a pounding headache. It wasn't fair for one person in the family to decide what was real and what wasn't.

"What's all the commotion?" Dad came out of the bedroom

dragging a bear-sized black suitcase, which he left looming by the front door. He was wearing flip-flops, khaki shorts, and a New York Yankees T-shirt that was so washed out you could barely read the letters. It creeped Melanie out that her father had clothes that were older than she was. She wondered if now that he was leaving he would buy some new clothes—or would he start his new life with a bunch of smelly old T-shirts and ink-smeared sweatpants?

"Nothing, David, no major catastrophe. You can go back to your packing. You have about twenty minutes before the moving guys get here." Dad ran his hand through what remained of his hair and glanced around the apartment, as though moving out had only just occurred to him. Half a dozen open boxes sat waiting to be filled with the contents of Dad's desk and bookshelves, boxes that had been sitting open in the living room for at least a week.

"Julia, can you take it down a notch, please? No one wants a fight today."

"You pay by the hour, you realize? Whatever you don't have organized, they're just going to throw into boxes, and there's a lot of stuff around the girls and I really need. How are the movers supposed to tell what's yours and what's ours? David, you really have to get your *shit* together!" Mom had started off speaking in her reasonable, you-know-I'm-right voice, but then gave up and started swearing, hands on her hips, color rising on her well-made-up cheeks. Melanie hated when her mother did that. She got in trouble for talking that way to Erika. It was one of a dozen ways her parents were both hypocrites. Their fights were louder and longer than any of Melanie and Erika's, and now they were breaking up for good. It wasn't like Melanie got to choose whether or not to live with Erika all those years.

Dad gave Mom one of his blank stares, as though he had no idea what she was saying. He looked around at his daughters for support. Jan and Erika turned away, both of them scrubbing out the now nearly invisible stain on Mom's carpet. Dad had been procrastinating packing all week. It had been bad enough with him sleeping on the couch. But then there was Mom, redecorating around him, and Dad, not even packing up his enormous stacks of color-coded files. Dad kept papers on every article and book he had ever written in his so-called study, which was really just a very large, very messy desk at the far end of the living room, behind a printed rice paper screen he'd sent back from Hong Kong on one of his trips. Now the living room was divided in half—with Mom's new furniture on one side, and Dad's half-packed boxes of books and folders on the other. The painted screen, with a red-lipped Asian woman on it, was the dividing line, and Melanie wondered who got to keep it.

"It's okay, Mom," Jan said. "We'll help Dad with the study." Jan disappeared into the kitchen and came back with a roll of packing tape and a pair of scissors. The night before, Dad had been in the kitchen packing his family's silver, but he still hadn't finished. He'd spent too much time calling them in to tell everyone about the gravy boat he had finally found, after misplacing it last Thanksgiving, or to tell them about the sugar bowl with the lion's head on it, and how his grandfather had brought it with him from Germany, the only piece of silver from his father's side of the family, which had been carried across Europe in their great-grandfather's backpack. *Why?* Melanie wanted to ask. Why did that make her father happy? That some man running for his life had nothing in the world he cared about more than a sugar bowl?

Jan took a large cardboard box from a stack against the wall and folded it into place, while Erika taped the sides down, smoothing the tape with the edge of her scissors. Jan was only slightly taller than Melanie, although she was three years older. But Melanie was the prettier of the two. Jan had narrow hazel eyes, while Melanie had large blue eyes, with dark lashes. Both Melanie and Jan were attractive, but Erika, on the other hand, was striking. Erika was one of those natural blondes with olive skin and hazel eyes—an unusual combination that, in itself, made her appearance intriguing. She also had the elongated limbs of a fashion model, and was so obviously that physical type that she had even been scouted for modeling work last year by a friend of Mom's in the fashion business. Erika had appeared in an ad that ran in all the major magazines, an accomplishment many girls her age could only dream of, but which was, for Erika, merely a curiosity, a way she happened to have spent an otherwise uneventful afternoon, a way to make some money to put away for college or graduate school, although with her talents she was likely to win scholarships to the top science programs in the country.

Erika, Melanie thought, was the main reason her life was not all it could be. Erika got on her nerves in a way she could not control, which in turn got her into trouble with Mom and Dad, both of whom worshipped Erika, and who were constantly on Melanie's case for her "anger issues." Erika was an irritating freak of nature who had somehow been born to Melanie's own parents.

Erika was unlike anyone else in the family—a giantess with a giant weirdo brain. Just looking at her sister could make Melanie's blood boil. Erika moved her long, dusky limbs in a quiet catlike manner, but she still somehow managed, mysteriously, to remain a total klutz. Of course, it was always Melanie's fault if she lost her temper or simply couldn't stand to be around her sister.

Watching Jan and especially Erika running around helping Dad pack made Melanie suddenly furious. She didn't think it was fair the way her father procrastinated, and then expected everyone to help him. She hated the way Erika doted on their father, when he was the one who was causing all their problems.

"Thanks, ladies," Dad said, smiling. "If you guys have that covered, Melanie can help me with the silver cupboard in here." Melanie knew this was coming, but still could not find it within herself to move.

"Yeah, right, I have about three hundred pages to read today," Melanie said. "Anyway, you should have packed it yourself, like Mom said."

Dad stared at her, his round-eyed, raccoon-looking stare.

Even Mom frowned, although Melanie was only taking her side. "Mel, I'm asking for your help. I'm moving out today, and I'd really appreciate it if this family could show me some consideration. I'm still your dad. This book is going to pay your college tuition, so you could get your ass in gear."

"David," Mom started, but Dad held up his hand. "It's what we agreed, Julia. I would stay here until Jan left for school, and we would be amicable about all of this. Melanie needs to understand. It's not some tragic divorce where everyone hates everyone. We all care about each other and take care of each other like always, but we're just choosing to live apart. No one's a bad guy. Now come give me a hand, Mel. It'll take half an hour."

From the other side of the room, Melanie could hear the *thunk, thunk* of Jan and Erika tossing one folder after another into boxes. Her mother busied herself with clearing the breakfast dishes and then disappeared into the bedroom. Melanie was beginning to doubt her mother had anywhere to go at all; she was just trying to act busy so she wouldn't have to help Dad. Melanie knew she should do what her father asked her, but somehow her body would not comply. If her father would stop staring at her, she might have been able to obey, but there was some coiled animal in her that she could not tame. She leaned back over her book. "No," she said. "I've got stuff to do." She hadn't intended to pick a fight, but a white sheet of anger had blanked out her brain, the way a computer screen is sometimes wiped clean by an otherwise undetectable surge of power. Something surged in Melanie's brain—a mood so far beyond her control it seemed to have a voice all its own.

Her father let out a deep sigh. "Melanie Russell, get your butt in here and help your dad before eight Russian dudes get here and turn this place inside out." Her father's face was turning red; even the top of his head was flushed. Jan and Erika kept their heads down, refusing to be drawn into her fight.

"If you're in such a rush, why are you wasting your time arguing with me?" Melanie said. It was as though her mouth had been taken over by aliens. She stared at her book. She had read the same sentence at least five times, and it still had not sunk in. She could feel the small hairs on the back of her neck rising. Her father sighed again.

"This is really disappointing behavior, Melanie. It's not the right tone at all. I'm leaving the country in two days, right after I drive Jan to school. Do you really want this to be the way you say good-bye?" His voice was less angry now than sad.

"I don't know, Dad," Melanie said. "I'm not the one doing all the yelling."

After that, the room stayed quiet, until forty-five minutes later when the doorman buzzed that the movers had arrived. By that time, Mom had left for a meeting, and Jan and Erika had packed Dad's desk, including, even, the yellow-glazed sculpture of a bird with big, black smudgy eyes that Melanie had made for Dad in first grade. Melanie had gotten dressed and retreated to her room to read, never having packed a single object. She had lost track of time, read a dozen or so pages, and then dozed off.

The bird was the first thing Melanie noticed was missing when she came out of her room—her little clay bird. It was impossible to think of it being stored away for a year in some storage locker, and even harder to think of it being unpacked in some entirely new place she would never live. Irrationally, she wanted to demand the bird be found, that they open every box until they located it, but it was too late. All the boxes were gone. If she had wanted to keep the bird sculpture safe until her father moved back from Hong Kong, she should have asked him hours ago.

As Mom predicted, the movers left a mess of dust and wads of packing tape strewn around the apartment. There were empty spaces, like scars, everywhere Dad's things had been—even in the coat closet, which had big gaps where Dad's winter parka, his never-worn ski jacket, and the tweed sports coat they all made fun of had recently hung.

Dad's study was now only a corner of the living room with nothing in it. The Chinese screen looked small and purposeless without a desk to conceal. When Dad left with Jan to meet the movers at his storage unit, he'd kissed Erika good-bye at the door, but Melanie had gone groggily to the dining table with her book, pretending, again, to read. "Good-bye, Mel," Dad had said, and he came over to her and kissed her on top of her head.

To her horror, fat tears rolled down her cheeks and onto the pages of her book. She wanted her fury back, and not this sudden, uncontrollable sadness. But these days she had no control over her feelings from one minute to the next, and her father's voice seemed to exacerbate the problem—exposing the rawest, most childlike parts of her personality. "We'll have breakfast before I go. I'll be staying at the Conrad when I get back from Providence, until my flight on Friday," Dad said quietly. Melanie nodded, and tried to speak, but only a humiliating croak came out. She didn't want to cry. She just wanted him to go. But just as strongly, she wanted everything in the apartment put back exactly the way it was—the old lamp, the old rug, and the dingy blue armchair.

Her father was infuriating, with his bossiness and his double standards. But she wanted to bury her face in his chest and cry the way she had when she was little and she'd fallen off her scooter on the asphalt path at Washington Market Park. Her father had sat there with her for a long time, patting her bloody knee, and never telling her, as her mother surely would have, to stop her crying, that she was okay, and it was only a scrape.

It was only later, after her father had left and the apartment was silent, that Melanie saw the yellow bird. It was behind the curtain at the far side of the living room where Dad had had his desk. For a moment, all she could do was stare at it. Had he left it behind on purpose? Because it was nothing? A worthless, ugly bit of painted clay? Or had he forgotten it, and it was something he'd have treasured? She could still grab it and run and try to catch him downstairs, where the movers were undoubtedly still loading the van. Melanie went to the window and looked down at the street below, but the angle was wrong, and she couldn't see the front of the building.

She picked up the bird sculpture and held it in her hand. It felt good and solid. She was numb now, neither sad nor angry, and so there was no reason to do what she did next: she wound up like a pitcher on the mound and threw the clay bird with all her strength across the room, so that it ricocheted off the far wall and bounced toward the front door, just as Erika was emerging from the bedroom. The bird narrowly missed Erika's head, and instead crashed into the bookcase by the front door, bouncing onto the flowered foyer rug, still intact, with only a small chip out of the top of its misshapen head.

"What was that for?" Erika asked, hand across her chest in a gesture of shock that reignited Melanie's anger.

"For everything," Melanie said. "For living." She didn't mean what she said, and hadn't even seen Erika coming, but she had no ready explanation for what she had done.

"What did I do?" Erika asked tearfully as Melanie picked up the bird and held it once more in her clenched fist.

"I don't know," Melanie said. "But you're doing it again."

There was no place to go. Erika was still dragging her things into Jan's old room, and from her bedroom Melanie could hear her sister muttering to herself, moving things into place until everything was perfect, the way Erika always needed them to be. The apartment was too quiet, and yet not quiet enough.

Melanie stormed into the kitchen and threw the clay bird into the garbage. There it lay on top of the leftovers from breakfast—soggy cereal and toast ends—though she figured, belatedly, the clay was probably recyclable. What she had wanted was to break something. Her hand still twitched and her heart still beat with the desire to do damage.

2

"**T**ime for the first-annual back-to-school Morris Foster birthday bash, and you lucky ladies are numbers one and two on my list," Morris said. "Free music, free drink, free love, all Morris Foster style. And the Big Daddy Dog, Foss Senior, will be there, too, so your moms can't say no. Friday night. Early, because I've got soccer in the a.m. No excuses accepted, that means you, Erika Russell."

Erika let Morris Foster and Binky Sanders, her two best friends and perennial science fair partners, corner her in the hall on her way to American history. She looked skeptically at Morris. Of course, she wanted to go to his birthday party, but she tried to avoid hanging out with Morris when he also had his jock friends around. Morris was brainy but athletic, someone who easily crossed social barriers at school, while Erika held closely to Binky and Morris. But this was junior year, Dad and Jan had both moved out of the house, and Erika had resolved to try to "be more normal," as she put it to herself. Mom and Melanie were the most normal people she knew, if "normal" meant people who were popular, went out a lot, and dressed cute every day of the week. Erika sometimes felt like a mutant in her own house. She knew her mother loved her, but Mom often looked at her with that bewildered "where did you come from?" look she never gave Melanie. Melanie, on the other hand, hardly gave Erika the time of day, unless it was to scowl at her for daring to borrow her purple sweater, while Melanie stole whatever she wanted from Erika's closet, without a word from Erika. Melanie's purple sweater was the only thing Erika ever took from Melanie, and she only took it for chess, because purple was lucky for chess.

"Seriously, Erika. No worries. The Big Man maintains a smoke-free castle, so any true partying is happening off-premises. No one blowing smoke up your virginal nasal passages, like at that thing at the park last year. Y'all remember that? How Erika tripped out on the *thought* of getting a contact high? Anyway, dude swears my ass is in a sling if he smells shit on any underage breath. I got to have my straight-edge people surrounding the Big Man, keeping him in the kitchen with the other oldies. Convince him all the ladies at RD are as boring as y'all."

"I'm definitely going," Binky said. "I already said during study hall. Come, Erika. It'll be fun, and it's at Morris's. You've been there a million times." Binky pouted, tossed her head, and stamped her foot like she was six. Binky was hard of hearing and still resorted sometimes to pantomime-like communication. In her early years at school, Binky had suffered socially for her disability and her husky voice, but in the last year Binky had become almost sought-after. She had straight blond hair, and full lips, and, unlike Erika, she enjoyed parties. Erika knew Binky would go to Morris's with or without her, even though she acted like she needed her.

The hallway was crowded with people changing classes, and Erika knew she'd have to make her decision quickly, or Morris would harass her for the rest of the day. Erika didn't smoke or drink. Unlike other people, she didn't even pretend to like these things. Morris said she should tell people she was a straight edger—a vegetarian, a drug-free punk—just to get people off her back, but Erika didn't even know what an "edger" was until Morris told her, and it seemed stupid to say she belonged to some sort of scene she'd never even heard of, especially if it meant getting a tattoo or a crazy haircut just to seem authentic. "That's cool, though," Morris had said. "No one else will know the edge scene either, but then they'll find like eighty-thousand edger sites, and you'll be the one who brought it to RD!"

Morris was always bringing new music or styles to their small downtown Manhattan private school. When they were in middle school, he'd listened to punk and dyed his hair red, and now he was all about jazz, and wearing old-school blazers with his jeans and dark, vintage glasses. But Erika was the opposite of Morris. Morris was a human chameleon. Erika was stuck in the prison of being Erika.

Erika had had wine before at home. Her mom and dad let her try it—two pretty full glasses last New Year's Eve. The first glass was like liquid happiness, a golden feeling that spread throughout her body. She thought then she understood what all the fuss was about. She'd drunk practically the entire second glass, and the feeling only got better. But almost immediately, a dullness followed, a gray dullness as huge as the golden feeling that came before it. Her body felt like lead, and her tongue became thick and clumsy, so it was hard to get the words out. She had decided after that that nothing should enter her body that changed the colors of her mind. Her mind took on strange, disturbing colors sometimes as it was, and she was afraid to make them any stranger.

"I guess I'm in," Erika said. "If your dad is there, we won't get in trouble. And if Binky deserts me for Christopher Primrose, it's only down the street and I can walk home myself." Binky shot Erika a sharp look, and Erika shrugged. Binky's nocturnal meetings with Christopher Primrose were supposedly secret. But that was only because Christopher wanted it that way, and avoided Binky at school. Morris shook his head.

"Live and let live, I always say. Girl likes a douche, that's cool. Takes all kinds," he said, winking at Binky. Binky hit him with her book bag, seeming to forget it was Erika who'd told her secret, and Morris waved his arms in the air in mock surrender.

Erika, Binky, and Morris Foster had been good friends for as long as Erika could remember, at least since Binky had transferred to RD from her uptown school in fourth grade. Kids uptown had been mean to Binky. They called her Deaf Barbie because she was nearly completely deaf, and she had blond hair she could almost sit on. Now, Binky's voice was clearer, and she'd gotten curvy, unlike Erika, whose body only knew one direction: up. It was okay with Erika that she wasn't as developed as either Binky or her younger sister, Melanie. Someone told her that for tall girls everything happened later. She worried, though, that more was missing from her than curves, and that being tall wasn't the only reason she didn't feel more like other girls.

———

The party was in two days, and Thursday would be busy, since they had a chemistry test Friday, so after school Erika and Binky went to Brenda Martin's in SoHo and chose outfits—things that were partyish, but not try-hard. Erika got a light-pink formfitting T-shirt dress that was looser on the top, blousing over a very tight lower half. It was short on Erika—grazing her upper thigh. Binky wanted to wear the same dress in black, but after seeing Erika in it, she chose a boxier dress—a black and white shift that looked good with ankle boots.

Erika loved the way she looked in the pink dress, so much so that she regretted having to take it off and change back into her regular T-shirt and jeans. When she got home, she showed it to her mother, and her mother had been so overcome with how good she looked, she took her right out to Century 21 to buy a pair of tan faux-suede boots to go with it. It wasn't often that Erika's mom approved of something she chose. Often Erika chose clothes for reasons other than how she looked in them.

This time, Erika had chosen well. The dress actually reminded her of strawberry meringue, her favorite sort of cookie, since it was made almost entirely of egg white. It was a kind of baking that was practically chemistry, the way the protein in the egg whites clung to the water molecules, which clung to fructose. The dress was colored like meringue and was clingy; it also happened to flatter her in every possible way, by chance really. The night of the party, her mother helped her with her makeup, and Erika felt transformed, but in a good way, as though the way she looked now was the way she was supposed to look always.

Erika was happy, a crystal-clear happiness, with no smoke or clouds in it. But then Melanie came out of the bathroom and stared opened-mouthed at Erika, as if she were some improbable creature. "You're letting her go to a party looking like that?" Melanie asked, as though she were the older sister, with a right to judge.

"She looks gorgeous—what's the problem, Melanie?" Mom responded.

Then Melanie said the thing that still rang in Erika's ears hours later. "She doesn't know how to *handle it*, Mom." Her mother had looked back at Melanie and waved her off, as if she didn't know what she was talking about. But Erica knew Melanie was right. There was some fundamental way in which who Erika looked to be was not who she really was.

———

At the party, Erika mostly hung out in the kitchen, where Morris had deposited her, and where Morris's dad was cooking and his stepmom was chatting with friends. Binky hung out in there for a while, too, helping Morris's stepmom lay out the snacks. Binky was good at making food look more attractive than it actually should. There were tricks for this, Erika learned, like the way Binky lined the guacamole bowl with a large piece of romaine lettuce, or the way she scattered dried cranberries and walnuts around the cheese platter, so they looked random but in fact were spread evenly, with no clumps of this or that. Randomness, Erika knew, had clumps.

Binky left to join the crowd in the other room. Although she never left Erika out, these days Binky moved comfortably through the cliques at school. This year, Erika had gained some attention from the same guys who hit on Binky, but usually, after the first few minutes of staring her up and down, they drifted away. It was easier to just talk to adults, which is what she was supposed to do at Morris's party, anyway.

Morris's dad, Foss, was in the kitchen with some old-style music on, some seventies stuff. He was drinking wine, enjoying his kid's party while not being in the thick of things. "What's up, Erika-girl—how's school treating you?" he asked. He was a big man, in his fifties, with light, coffee-colored skin and a deep voice. He had been a movie actor when he was young, and now directed movies and TV shows. He was one of the most famous parents at the school. Erika had once seen him in an old movie about a jazz singer, and she had been startled and slightly alarmed at watching someone she knew pretend to be someone else, as though acting were some sort of psychiatric illness. Poor Foss, she'd felt, had been crammed into the idea of someone else, betrayed by his own face.

"I like this year better than ninth or tenth. The new science lab is awesome, and we have three choices for lunch," Erika replied. She liked Foss, and felt comfortable with him, even though he was famous. Erika's mother often complained about the big egos of people in fashion, and the stars she occasionally interviewed. Julia claimed that fame made people bitter about having to go on being people.

"Oh yeah, gotta have choices for lunch, that's what I always say!" Foss laughed and slapped Erika on the back as if she had said something intentionally funny. But then he stopped talking and looked at her for a moment. She had her hair up in a high ponytail, which set off her cheekbones. Her mother had made her eyes up so they stood out against her slightly olive skin. For a moment, she looked like Julia Roberts, only with a narrower nose—and prettier. "You ever do any acting, Erika-girl? You're always behind the stage when Morris is up there hamming it up in those school plays—but do you ever act?"

"No, I haven't," Erika said. "I modeled, though. A friend of my mom's got me an agent."

"Well, there you go. But you look like an actor, to me." Morris's dad still stared at Erika, and she was beginning to feel herself flush all over.

"I think being an actor seems really hard," Erika said,

looking down, remembering Foss in the movie.

Morris's dad laughed and slapped his knee. "Erika-girl, that's what I like about you! Most people think acting is the easiest job there is—just playing for a living—but you're right. It's hard, if you're any good—and knowing that it's hard is probably the first step to being any good. You should think about it."

"No. I don't think so. I liked modeling, though, because you can just focus on one thing—like a body part or something—and then stay that way. I can stand still a really long time—the fashion director liked that about me." Erika found herself striking a pose as she spoke. She was standing between Foss's leather barstool and the cooking island where Binky had set out all the food.

It was then, as she held her head high and stared in a far-off way, that she noticed one of the other men in the kitchen staring at her. It was Morris's half brother, Jason, who was also in the movie business. Unlike Morris, Jason was half white, and he had long curls that hung almost to his shoulders. He had very dark eyes, so it was difficult to distinguish pupil from iris, and his lashes were long and curled so he looked somehow like a very large, very happy infant, the type of baby everyone wanted to hold, jiggle, and make laugh.

"You can't keep all the pretty girls to yourself, Foss," Jason said, stepping toward the island that was between him and Erika, and shaking his head so his curls skimmed his shoulders. Erika had met Jason once at a birthday party years before, but he didn't seem to remember. He was in college when they were in elementary school, so they'd just been kids to him. He called his dad Foss, as everyone else did, which was short for Foster—Morris's last name.

"Oh, this one here is special—she's my girl, Erika, been my girl since maybe third grade, right, sweetheart?" Morris's dad winked at her. It was true, she'd always talked to Morris's dad at parties and at school events. He seemed, unlike most people, to find her amusing.

Jason leaned across the island and narrowed his baby eyes at her, pretending to try to determine what was so special about her. "You're right—she is special. And tall. Care for a bite?" Jason picked up a tray of mini hot dogs wrapped in pasty-looking dough and smiled a little too broadly, as though he were making a not-very-funny joke and needed to compensate for it by grinning.

"No thanks," Erika said. "Those look like they once had a face."

Jason looked at her a moment, perplexed, and then back at the mini hot dogs. "Yo, man, that's kinky. I like that," he said. Erika blushed. She wasn't sure exactly what Jason was talking about, but she had the uncomfortable feeling she got sometimes when people around her said dirty-sounding things. "I've been off meat for two years now," Erika said, still blushing. "It's totally impossible for me to choke something like that down."

Jason laughed and smacked his chest with his own fist. When he started to say something else, Foss interrupted him. "Cut it, Jay. She's just a kid." Foss's voice was stern suddenly, not jokey, but like a dad whose kid had crossed the line. Jason looked up, startled. "Chill, Dad, I'm just having a little fun here." But Morris's dad shook his head gravely and Jason walked out of the room. Erika knew Foss had been trying to protect her, but her heart sank a little as she watched Jason retreat. She had liked the shadow his eyelashes cast on his smooth cheek, and the way the cheek held at its center an equally smooth dimple.

———

Morris's party had been nice, but unnerving. Binky disappeared for a long time with Christopher Primrose. With Binky missing, and Foss getting into a grouchy mood over something Erika wasn't quite sure of, Erika spent most of her time with Morris and a couple of other kids she knew from the Rube Goldberg club. They had fun talking about the time they went to Boston and Erika and Morris won the Rube Goldberg competition, even though Erika had to take a barrette out of her hair to get the paper-stapling machine to actually work. You weren't supposed to add any elements to your design during the competition, but Erika had stealthily hidden the barrette under a complex web of rubber bands. No one knew, not even Evan, the science teacher—if he had, he would have had to tell the organizers, and they'd have been disqualified. That quick thinking with the barrette had been Erika's claim to fame in seventh grade.

Fortunately, after another twenty minutes or so, Binky appeared, slightly disheveled, and she and Erika left Morris's to be sure they'd be back at Erika's by eleven. Binky was quiet during the walk home, and Erika noticed her lips had a slightly crushed look to them. She wondered what it was like kissing Christopher Primrose, but she couldn't begin to imagine. He had a very dry-looking face. She didn't think she'd like touching him.

After the night of Morris's party, Binky kept coming up with more nighttime plans. Often, the parties involved Christopher Primrose, but when Erika asked Binky if they were going out, she was bitchy. "You have to stop telling people about me and Chris," she had demanded. The fact was, though, at Rose Dyer High School there were no secrets, and other people had already begun to talk about Binky.

One boy, Jacob Weinrib, had said Binky was a "superfreak" and encouraged his friend Timmy Saltz to invite her to his party, a fact Erika learned in chess strategy from Tim's lab partner, Mark. Erika had been called a freak by those boys before, but superfreak was a new one. She knew it had to do with sex, but wasn't sure what type of act it referred to. She thought she might ask Melanie, but then she had forgotten about the whole thing. Whatever it did mean, the result was that Erika went to more parties, which was okay with her now that she had gotten used to it. There were usually kids to hang with who she knew, and she especially liked dressing up in pretty clothes. She liked the way her mom paid attention to her on those nights, and did her hair for her, like she did Melanie's when Melanie went out.

Often, when she wanted to talk about important stuff to her mom, like science fair, or chess club, her mom seemed distracted. But her mother always smiled when it was time to dress for a party, smiled in a way that reached up to her eyes, which got squinty and sparkly, like happy-face eyes in a little kid's drawing, or a picture in a magazine. Only Erika knew now that those really smiley people in the magazines had to hold those smiles for unnaturally long periods of time. She knew those real-looking smiles could be worn, without any feeling at all, almost indefinitely. She wondered how all the happy-looking people really felt at all the parties they went to, and she tried not to be afraid of them.

3

When Jan Russell's roommate, Eliza Smith, arrived in the late afternoon of Jan's first day on campus, Jan thought there had been a mistake. She had taken Brown's roommate-survey seriously. She had already met Andy Berg at freshman orientation. Andy was from the New York City suburbs, and when they chatted Jan had been immediately hopeful that she had just met her first real college friend. Eliza Smith, on the other hand, was not what she had expected in a roommate. Eliza Smith was unlike anyone Jan had ever met before, much less lived with.

"Monster fucking traffic," Eliza exclaimed as she burst into the dorm room. She carried a large green duffel bag on her shoulder. Her head was shaved to the scalp on one side, and her hair was dyed a dark, purplish red. She had light freckles, blue eyes, a round, girlish face, and was tall, with an ample figure. But any feminine attributes were overshadowed by her eyebrow piercing, knee-high combat boots, fishnet stockings, black short-shorts, and a T-shirt that read *The Patriarchy Won't Fuck Itself.*

Jan found herself reading and rereading the T-shirt slogan several times. She knew she was being overly literal, but she couldn't decide whether the declaration was supposed to be a positive or negative statement. She made a mental note to ask her boyfriend, Adam, what he thought, when they spoke at the end of the week. Jan and Adam hadn't broken up before leaving for college, but they had decided to sever electronic ties. They'd talk once a week on Saturday mornings, but they wouldn't text or use social media to keep in touch. Above all, they wouldn't talk, text, or chat as a substitute for having actual, in-person college experiences.

The electronic separation had been Adam's suggestion, but Jan had readily agreed. She didn't want to be one of those girls who was basically in a relationship with her phone. She didn't want to "introduce" Adam to her new friends by having them text each other. There was something cliché and high-school-seeming about the whole idea of everyone you knew knowing each other online and through chats. Still, it was hard to resist the temptation to snap a picture of Eliza. It would take weeks to describe to Adam what a single image could reveal about Jan's new roommate.

Eliza's possessions had arrived in the room earlier in the day, in creased, used-looking boxes, sent by a shipping company from Montana. Jan had glanced at them and wondered what sort of girl would follow the sloppily duct-taped, beat-up boxes.

Most of the other kids in the dorm had parents with them for move-in day, and new-looking luggage—suitcases on wheels, trunks with shiny latches. Eliza, however, arrived without a parent in tow, and she carried a bag that Jan thought smelled a bit like horses.

The only fortunate thing was that by the time Eliza Smith arrived, Jan's father, David, had finally left. He'd insisted on helping Jan set up her computer and printer, a task she could have done easier without him there, swearing under his breath with every step of the process. He'd been high-maintenance all day. He'd asked Jan a dozen times whether she was annoyed with him for leaving for Hong Kong so soon after she arrived at Brown, but he had avoided the more significant topic of his separation from Mom. Dad was a great one for talking about everything that didn't matter.

"Hi! Need help with that?" Jan offered, trying to be friendly. "Did you take a cab all the way from the airport?"

"A what?" Eliza said. "No, no, no. Greyhound."

"That must have been long," Jan said, taken aback, thinking Eliza meant she had taken a bus all the way from Montana. But then Eliza clarified.

"Let's see. I began my odyssey east on Tuesday. Airbus out of Kalispell heading west, naturally, to Seattle. All eastern travel in this country seems to begin by heading west. Layover. Two hours of fighting off this unusually persistent pervert. First the guy wanted to buy me a cupcake. Then Starbucks. Then pizza. He thought I was some teen runaway he was going to sell into white slavery or some shit. Finally told him, 'How about get me an extra-hot latte so I can pour it on your balls?' I am a basic perv magnet. Then in Houston some army dude sits down next to me, takes out his laptop, gets on this site that's like International Warehouse of Bondage Toys. I like toys, I mean who doesn't, but this is the airport, guy. There's grandmothers here.

"When I finally land at Logan it's like eight planes are all getting bags at the same carousel. It's an absolute crush of people slinging giant bags everywhere, and who gets felt up? A handful of my ass fat is totally palmed, but I can't tell who it is. Everyone around me is looking entirely focused on their bags, and I am like, right, my ass looked exactly like your wife's Louis Vuitton. Jesus.

"Then I stayed with my aunt in Boston. My mom's sister, who I met once when I was five. She has eleven cats. She works in an adolescent psych ward, and she is a psycho-bitch cat lady. She had no food at all in her house but cat food and Lucky Charms, which if you think about it look like cat kibbles.

"Then on the Greyhound I sit next to a dude who must've weighed four hundred pounds. No shit. He kept taking these sandwiches out from God knows where. Turkey club. Italian combo. Tuna. Egg salad. Fluffernutter. A total sandwich-obsessed freak. I was like, man, I know actual hogs that maintain weight at fewer calories. But at least he was just a sandwich perv."

Jan tried not to appear shocked, but she could feel her mouth go slack and she knew she was staring. "Wow," she finally responded. "That's a lot more eventful than my car ride with my dad. Only thing that happened to us was the GPS directions in the rental car were all in German. My dad speaks German and about five other languages really badly."

Jan couldn't help but feel that she could have done more to make this story amusing, that there was some vivid detail she could have added to capture how funny it had been with her father speaking German back to the GPS voice, something that would make Eliza think she was remotely interesting, but she felt tongue-tied and overwhelmed. As Eliza turned her attention to unpacking, an uncomfortable silence descended on the room. Jan knew she was overreacting, that this was only first-day-of-school jitters, but she knew herself well enough to know she needed to take a walk and regain perspective.

It was frightening how natural it seemed to want to talk to Adam. They had seen each other almost every day for the past year. But there was no way Jan was going to be the first to break the electronics ban. She forced herself to act busy organizing her clothes and desk, and then as soon as it seemed polite, she excused herself to see whether Andy Berg, the girl from the New York City area, was around.

To Jan's relief, Andy was standing in front of her room, struggling to get her key out of the lock. "This is the tenth stupid thing I've done since I saw you," Andy said. "Worst so far was slamming the window on my finger." Andy held out her sloppily bandaged pinky. "My roommate, Sarah, attempted to help me out, but she is apparently a germ- and bodily-fluids-phobe, so this was not a great first moment together."

"Ha," Jan laughed, and nudged Andy aside, then gently wiggled Andy's key free from the lock. "My special talent," Jan said. "Comes from being the oldest in a dysfunctional, apartment-dwelling family. Someone needs skills."

"Really?" Andy said. "You're that one? I have two older brothers and have basically been carried on people's shoulders my entire life. My parents and my older brother, Craig, literally unpacked all my shit. It was totally embarrassing. Sarah was there all by herself arranging her deodorizers and antiseptic sprays, and my whole family was micromanaging my dresser. My mother is a folding guru. She teaches classes on how to fold stuff. Apparently it's the key to happiness. My brother and my dad are both architects, so that's more of the same. I, on the other hand, am a brat in recovery. They sent *me* to a therapist because they were so concerned that I was a senior in high school and I left my smelly gym clothes in the car. In my OCD family, mess is a psychological condition."

Jan smiled. "Sounds like you're the Melanie of your family. That's my baby sister. She's a sophomore in high school. But I'm sure you're better adjusted than Melanie. She's growing out of it, but she's sort of a mean girl. I think she might tell people where to sit at lunch."

"Oh, that's not me," Andy said. "I'm harmless. I just have zero life skills. No sense of direction. Failed my driver's test three times. That sort of thing." They left the dorm together and headed across the small green toward the main part of campus. The sun felt good on Jan's face, and she breathed deeply and tried to relax. So what if she had to live with someone she had nothing in common with? She was having an actual conversation, at least, with a real person, someone she related to. Andy stopped for a moment and twisted her long, curly dark hair into a bun, took a yellow pencil from her jeans pocket, and stuck it through her hair. To Jan's amazement, the heavy bun stayed perfectly in place.

"Well, at least you're good with hair," Jan said. She felt her own thin blond hair flat against the back of her neck. She'd wanted to get it cut before she left New York, but things were so chaotic at home with both her and her father moving out, she didn't get a chance.

"Yeah," Andy said. "I did inherit the perfection gene in this one area. I can cut hair, too. I cut my own all the time. One summer a couple years ago I learned how from watching about a thousand YouTube videos.

"Really?" Jan said. "I was just thinking how I wanted to buy a pair of scissors and just start cutting." Jan had always wanted to be one of those girls who cut their own hair, or had a friend dye it some unnatural color. That was Eliza, though, not her. Pathetically, she'd always gone to her mother's stylist in Tribeca.

"Oh, shit, yeah," Andy said, looking at Jan. "I would love to give you one of those layered bobs. Would you do it? Your hair would be great for that, maybe with long bangs? Your hair has to be perfectly straight. Otherwise bangs don't work. Most people have some little wave in front they don't even notice until it's too late."

They had been walking around the quad too absorbed in their conversation to pay much attention to where they were going. Jan looked up for the first time and took in their surroundings. There were groups of students sitting on the steps in front of the student center, and other kids hanging out on the quad listening to music on giant headphones. There was one girl playing the ukulele, sitting with a pink-haired girl wearing motorcycle boots and a pompom hat—styles Jan envied and disdained at the same time. *Posers*, she thought. They were everywhere, and Jan again fought the impulse to snap a picture. It was scary how much she wanted to show Adam everything at Brown—not everything, really, just the annoying parts. She wasn't sure what that said about her, or their relationship, but she doubted it was good. She took a deep breath. There was a part of her that knew she was being ridiculous. This wasn't high school. It didn't matter as much anymore what people wore. In college, you could be whoever you wanted.

It was a warm, sunny day and campus was crowded, although only freshman were supposed to be moving in. Jan figured a lot of upperclassman had arrived back just for this moment—to hang out before the grind of school officially began. On the upper quad, some shirtless guys were kicking a soccer ball. One of them had long, straight hair that fell into his eyes, and abs he kept touching in that way guys with really good bodies have of drawing attention to themselves without seeming to realize it. Why, Jan wondered, was she one of those people who, no matter what she did, seemed to be making too much of an effort?

Everywhere Jan looked everyone seemed hip and stylish. Brown girls seemed to all be skinny, or at least comfortable in their skin. Lots of kids were barefoot, or wearing Birkenstocks or Docs with cutoffs and droopy, off-the-shoulder cropped tops. It seemed like everyone had a piercing or a tattoo. It wasn't how Jan remembered campus from her tour. There had been preppy kids, science nerds, and just normal-seeming people.

The more she looked around, the more the idea of letting Andy cut her hair seemed like a good one. She was here, finally—away from home. She needed to start to take more risks. She needed to stop thinking about Adam, and what he'd think of her every move. She needed to stop *thinking* so hard about things that hardly mattered, things that were supposed to be fun—meeting people and making friends. She glanced back at the soccer-playing boys. A short, dark-haired boy had scored a goal and was racing around the quad jumping on his teammate's backs. A light-skinned black guy dodged him and both boys went tumbling to the ground. A boy in a gray tank sat down on the grass and watched the other guys rolling around in the dirt, shaking his head in mild amusement. Maybe that was how the world was really divided, Jan thought, between people who knew how to have a good time, and the people who watched.

———

Jan stared into Andy's mirror. Hair was strewn all over the white porcelain sink, which was identical to the sink in Jan's room. The snips of dirty-blond hair were darker, mousier than

Jan had expected. Maybe she should color her hair as well? But that would have to wait for another night. They were already too buzzed to be doing what they were doing.

They'd each had a couple beers before Andy had begun cutting. Classes had started a few days before, but it was a short week and this was how Jan and Andy were celebrating their first Friday evening in college. They had met after class on the quad, gone to CVS to get hair shears, and then walked down to Sheldon Street to buy beer with Andy's fake ID.

Jan's hair wasn't salon-perfect, but that was the point. It came out a little uneven—shorter in the back than the front, and Andy kept trying to even it all out, which meant she cut it shorter than she'd planned—nearly up to Jan's chin—but the bangs came out better than Jan had imagined, long and fringe-like, so her eyes took on a much deeper green. The bangs made Jan look sexier, less fresh-faced, almost, Jan thought, a little French.

When Jan went back to her room to grab a sweater, Eliza, who'd just gotten up from a late-afternoon nap, had been impressed. "Holla," she'd said. "There's a hottie on the hall." Jan laughed and ran back to Andy's room feeling carefree and sure of herself for the first time since she'd arrived at Brown.

Now, Andy had produced a joint. Jan took it and inhaled, as though she smoked every day. The fact was, Jan had only smoked pot a few times before. Adam hated the pothead kids at RD, hated the way kids came to class stoned, as though their parents had spent all that money on private school to have their kids go to school wasted out of their brains.

Jan tossed her head and felt the bare back of her neck. "My God, I can't believe how short it is," she said, laughing.

"Edgy," Andy replied, taking a long hit on the joint.

"Speaking of edgy, Andy, what do you think of Eliza? My roommate?" Jan asked. Jan hadn't wanted to gossip about Eliza, but was talking to a friend about your roommate gossip? Or was it natural, like complaining about the weather?

"Ballsy. That chick is so ballsy. You know we're in class together? The Dialectics of Images?"

"She told me," Jan said.

Andy nodded, holding her breath, and then exhaling a long steady stream of smoke. "There's this unbelievably beautiful dude in the class. An upperclassman, maybe a junior. Eliza and I are the only freshmen. Eliza flirts so much with this guy. He had this whole theory about why people buy stainless steel refrigerators based on this one ad from the *Times*. He went on about beauty and machinery and capitalism. It was pretty genius, how the guy put it. I thought the stainless steel just made everything like a mirror.

"Anyway, Eliza went right up to the guy after class, pointed at him, and said "I think you are fucking brilliant, Mr. Stainless." He was completely dumbfounded. I think she'd have a chance with him, too, but he has a girlfriend. I've seen him hugging this redhead with really long dreads on the quad."

Jan sighed. She was sure that Eliza thought she was boring, conventional. Adam, she was sure, would judge her for smoking, and Andy for getting her high. Her mother would think she looked chubbier already, and Dad would be worried her classes weren't challenging enough. What would her sisters think? Melanie and Erika always thought she was the perfect sister, she knew that. But that wasn't the real her either. People were supposed to "find themselves" at college, but was this how they did it? By questioning everything they thought they were?

4

The Perilous Thongs were Melanie and Jess's favorite band, even though most of their songs were about college life and contained obscure references to eighties music, two things neither of them knew much about. Still, the PTs were hugely popular due to their peppy pseudo-reggae sound. Their best song by far was "Some Kinda Feeling," which was the song the band derived its name from. "You know it's some kinda feelin', when you're wearin' your perilous thong!" Who didn't like that line? All the kids at Rose Dyer were into the PTs, but Melanie and Jess were the truly lucky ones. Jess's dad Rick had a client he trained who was the band's attorney. Jess was famed at RD for having two complete sets of gay parents—a mom who was a yoga teacher, and another mom who was a banker, and then a dad who was a lawyer, and Rick, who was a personal trainer. No one was supposed to know who Jess's biological parents actually were, but Jess had a pert little nose just like Rick, and strawberry-blond hair like Sara, the yoga teacher.

Rick had scored front-row tickets and backstage passes for Jess and Melanie for the PT's show at the Bang Bang Room. Melanie was so pumped up for the show, it didn't even matter that they had to go with a grown-up—and even so, Rick scarcely mattered.

Rick's truly adult status was questioned even by Melanie's mom, but Rick finally won her over when the two of them ran into each other at back-to-school night. "Julia," Rick had said, "do you realize who the Perilous Thongs are? They're the Who, they're the Clash, they're the Police—I mean, this is absolutely epic for the kids, you've got to let me take them—I'll literally put a leash on them!" Julia had wrinkled her nose up at that, and said, "Um, Rick, no leash, okay?" And that was how the thing was settled. That was how Melanie and Jess ended up sitting next to Rick at the Bang Bang Room in the front row, practically looking up the vaguely aristocratic, curved nostrils of the PTs' lead singer, Peter Todd. No one knew if that was the guy's actual name, but it went with his whole retro-preppy style.

The crowd was hopping and all three of them had been stoked since the first song. What Rick didn't know was that Jess had a flask of vodka stashed in the inside pocket of her leather jacket, and that she'd spiked her and Melanie's lemonades at home, and she'd just poured a shot in each of the girls' Sprites. Melanie was having trouble choking the drink down, since Jess poured so much vodka in it. Melanie had, on several occasions, sipped more wine than her mother might have noticed at family events. When her grandfather was around it was easy, since he always offered it to her. Her mom's dad seemed to enjoy family parties, and never minded when everyone pushed the limit. This was different, though; this was vodka, and Melanie wasn't sure Jess knew what she was doing. At least with wine, you could tell how much you'd had to drink. When your friend just kept dropping some clear, deadly liquid into your Sprite, who knew?

Jess was actually beginning to look a little strange, a little pale, and a little green. At first Melanie thought it was just the lighting. It was near the end of the show, and the crowd was on its feet, moving as one, but Jess kept banging into Melanie, and it didn't seem like it was on purpose, more like she was losing her balance. Finally, during the encore, when the PTs were really ripping into a new, very catchy song, Jess sank down into her seat and put her head between her knees. Then, right there in the front row, she puked out a whole mess of yellowish liquid. Melanie even thought she saw Peter Todd's eyes widen as he let out one of his trademark yelps, but then she figured he was probably blinded by the lights.

Melanie felt pretty sober after Jess lost it; once Rick was in on what was going on, she snapped to. As they maneuvered through the crowd, with Jess bouncing between them, Rick gave her the third degree. "Where the heck did you two get the liquor?" He seemed more curious than angry. Melanie shrugged.

"That was Jess's department. I was supposed to get us a joint, but I failed," Melanie confessed. Why not? Rick wouldn't care.

"Did you now? Was that due to a lack of knowledge, or will?" Rick asked.

"Both. I thought Gerald was getting it from this guy kids buy from at McDonald's, but then he lamed out. And I didn't want to go and get some on the street—who knows what those guys are selling?"

"Right, better safe than sorry. Everyone knows you've got to buy your pot at Mickey D's." Rick was getting pretty worked up now, shaking his head and talking in a snotty, sarcastic way. Rick gestured toward Jess's wobbly head. "Now, look at me," Rick said as he tried to hail a cab. "It appears to all the world like I got my own daughter totally wasted in public—maybe you guys should have thought of that, huh? The predicament your plans put me in—after all I did for you getting tickets, and backstage passes you couldn't even use?"

Rick seemed particularly annoyed about the passes going to waste, and Melanie wanted to say something that would make him feel better, but nothing came immediately to mind. "Sorry, Rick," she finally said, sounding like a little kid. "Next time, we'll be more careful."

Rick looked at her and shook his head. "That's not exactly the answer I was looking for, sweetheart. You're supposed to say there won't be a next time."

"Yeah, but would you even believe that if I said it?" Rick didn't seem like the kind of dad who would want to hear the usual bullshit lines. Melanie wasn't even sure if her own father would want her to swear to *never* drink or smoke.

"No, I guess not, but you guys are really still little kids, Mel. Don't be in such a hurry to grow up, okay?"

Rick was one of the only grown-ups outside her own family who ever called her Mel, and it always struck her as odd, as if there were something he knew about her—some secret. Anyway, for all he was telling her not to be in a hurry to do grown-up stuff, he was there in the cab talking to her as if she weren't a fifteen-year-old full of booze. Shouldn't he be furious, dropping her off at her house and telling her mother what happened? No, he seemed to be taking the cool-Rick approach to the whole ordeal. They were headed back to Jess's apartment, to get Jess tucked in.

Once Jess was safe in bed, after puking one more time, this time at least in the toilet, Rick made Melanie a bowl of bowtie pasta with butter and cheese. He hadn't wanted her to go to bed with just liquor in her gut. Melanie felt like a little kid, sitting on a stool in Jess's kitchen, eating kid food. Jess's other dad was working late even though it was a Saturday night—he had a big deal going on, so it was just herself and Rick. Finally, after finishing her pasta, Melanie asked Rick what he was going to say to Julia.

"I am going to tell your very respectable mother that you hold your booze way better than my kid."

"Really?" Melanie was disappointed—she thought maybe Rick would let the whole thing blow over.

"Yep. Look, kid, she has a right to know. If Jess got wasted at your place, your mom would tell us, no doubt." Rick suddenly looked older, standing in his kitchen, eating pasta out of the bowl with his fingers. He was buff and good-looking in that gay-guy way, but he was pretty old, just the same. His freckles had a faded look to them, as did his still-thick brown hair. Melanie wondered what it was that made people seem to fade that way. Were their skin cells actually wearing out, or was it something more mysterious, some life force that dimmed in them?

"My mom is pretty stressed right now, with my dad gone and all." Melanie pouted. She knew she was playing the fucked-up family card, maybe even exaggerating her own distress, but then again, hadn't she a right to a misstep or two? Her parents' marriage had blown up basically right in front of her. Couldn't everyone cut her a little slack? "Mom might kind of flip out on me. She already thinks I'm the evil one at home, and Erika is like a teen goddess." Melanie felt a pounding headache coming on, and she wondered why it was people liked to drink so much. It'd been fun for a while at the concert, but she'd felt pretty woozy since getting in the cab. The food helped, but still—her head was heavy and throbbing, like it felt one time when she'd had a bad flu. It made it difficult to think straight, difficult to gauge the effect her words were having on Rick.

"Well, I don't think you're evil, Mel. You're more like strong-willed, like one of those tough broads in an old movie—like Ingrid Bergman in *Notorious*."

"You mean that big-nosed actress?"

"Yeah, I guess you could call her that."

"I saw that movie! She's a total slut, but then she catches all those Nazis in the end!" Melanie thought for a moment about the comparison to herself. It was neither flattering nor insulting, but it intrigued her that she might fall into a category—a type. She was kind of tough, not one to lose control, like Jess. She supposed she had it in her to be like Ingrid Bergman's character—someone who could even marry a man she didn't love, who she hated even, just to spite the guy she did love. But was spite such an admirable trait?

Later, when she was unsuccessfully trying to get to sleep in Jess's trundle bed, Melanie thought about what Rick said, and she had to admit, he kind of had her right, because Melanie did often feel angry and spiteful. Maybe it was since Dad had gone away, or since Jan went to college, or Erika got so beautiful. She couldn't really say what motivated her. The truth was, Melanie didn't really feel sorry for Jess for getting sick. She was pissed that she had to go and ruin what should have been an unbelievable night. Now, when Gerald asked about going backstage and meeting the Thongs, Melanie would have to tell him the dismal truth—things hadn't gone according to plan. There was no hanging out with the band, no getting close enough to Peter Todd to determine, as she'd often wondered, whether his flashing white teeth were real, or some sort of stagy prosthetics. No, all she got in the end was a lecture from Rick and the stink of Jess's puke breath keeping her up half the night. She could only hope that the repercussions wouldn't be too severe. It was fall, after all. There was Halloween coming soon, and then the holidays, and it would suck if her mom was on her case just as the school year got rolling.

5

Adam looked lost standing at the bus stop on the corner of Thayer and Waterman. Jan knew she was late, having pointlessly changed her clothes three times. What she wore was nothing special—jeans, a chunky sweater, and her old tan Sperry's. She'd decided dressing up for Adam's visit would seem awkward and that the best approach was to pretend they were still the same low-key couple they'd been when they met each other every morning in the RD cafeteria for tea and bagels. At one point, Adam looked directly at Jan as she hurried breathlessly up the block, but he failed to return her wave. He didn't seem to recognize her.

Jan slowed to a more casual pace and studied Adam from afar. Five weeks at school hadn't changed him. Adam was tall and narrow-shouldered without being skinny. He was wearing worn, off-white Converse, jeans, and a button-down shirt with the tails untucked. He had a blue sweatshirt over one shoulder, as the day had become warm for October. Jan felt her heart skip a beat.

Adam finally looked Jan's way and broke into a wide grin. She had almost reached the bus stop—and he walked the few steps over to her with his long, loping strides, and put his arms around her.

"Holy shit, I almost didn't recognize you! Your hair!" Adam kissed her on the mouth, and began inspecting her head from every angle. She felt her doubts slip away.

"You like?" Jan tilted her head slightly, in a way she thought made her look especially cute.

"It's nice, like what's-her-face, from that movie . . ."

"Rachel Altman?"

"Exactly."

Jan knew Adam would think she looked like Rachel Altman, and in fairness to him, the comparison was not far off. It was a compliment, but Jan couldn't help but think it was really about her small eyes. Obviously Rachel Altman's worst feature as well. The bangs looked good, because without them it always looked like she was squinting.

Adam kept his arm around Jan's shoulders and surveyed the scene. "So, where's a good place to eat? I'm starving."

"Didn't you eat breakfast?" Jan asked, disappointed that Adam's first thought was about food, and not about being alone with her. She had asked Eliza earlier in the week if she could let her have the room for the weekend. Eliza had laughed about being "sexiled," but Jan didn't feel guilty. Eliza often didn't come back to the room at night.

"Yeah, I had an omelet at the student union, but that was hours ago. Is there any place around here that doesn't cost ten bucks for a sandwich?" Adam asked.

It was something about Adam that Jan had almost forgotten. Even though Adam's parents owned a large Upper West Side apartment, he couldn't bear to spend any money; he got her gifts, but the small things—pizza, lunch, random stuff—he had always complained about buying.

"Well," Jan replied, "just about everything on the hill is pricey—unless you want D'Angelo's—which is a grease bomb."

"Sure," Adam said, "I'll take my chances."

Jan stared at the menu at D'Angelo's while the thin, blond girl at the counter waited. Jan couldn't bring herself to get a foot-long sandwich. Her jeans were feeling snug at the waist. "Chicken salad," Jan said, finally, "blue cheese on the side." The counter girl looked at Adam, but Adam still stared up at the menu.

"Are you together?" the girl asked.

"Oh, no—I mean, you've got cash?" Adam said, glancing at Jan, obviously waiting for Jan to pay for her own order.

"Oh, sure," Jan said. At home, she and Adam had usually taken turns paying. She felt panicked for a moment. Maybe their relationship status wasn't what she'd thought? Maybe the electronic breakup was a sign Adam was giving that things weren't the same—a sign she'd missed?

They took their plastic trays and sat at a table by the window that looked out over Thayer Street. Jan managed to choke down a few bites of watery-looking chicken salad. She was determined not to be upset by what happened at the counter. "Oh, look," she said suddenly, pointing out the window. "There she is!"

"Who?" asked Adam.

"Eliza! My legendary roommate. You won't meet her, most likely. I asked if she could stay somewhere else. Obviously," Jan said, blushing. But Adam ignored her implication.

"Where? I feel cheated not meeting the most radicalized freshman at Brown." Adam leaned around Jan to see where she was pointing.

"Right there across from the Ben and Jerry's. She's not the one with dreads." Jan said.

Adam nodded. He seemed impressed. "Who's the other one?" he asked.

"Oh, that's some sophomore, I think. Eliza's friends with all these sophomores and juniors. You have to hand it to her. She really hit the ground running." Jan knew she sounded sarcastic, although she really did admire Eliza.

Adam looked thoughtful. "Is that what you want to be?" he asked suddenly.

"What?" asked Jan, defensive.

"Well, with the hair and everything. Are you going hipster now? Trying to look more like her?" he said, gesturing toward the corner where Eliza and her friend stood.

Jan frowned, hurt. "It's just a haircut," she said quietly.

"I didn't say I didn't like it. I do. I'm just asking because it seems like a departure," Adam insisted.

Jan sighed. "Maybe it is a bit," she said. "I always wanted to do something like this. But you know how my mom is. She acts like not going to the best stylist in the city is a form of suicide."

Adam raised his eyebrows. "So you *are* turning into a little rebel," he said. "Not that I blame you. Your mom's kind of a snob. Her and your crazy little sister." Adam laughed and shook his head. "I always wondered why your mom let your sisters go at it like that. They had some pretty intense brawls."

The conversation had taken an unfortunate turn. Jan regretted criticizing her mother. What Adam said about Melanie and Erika was true, but Adam was an only child and his parents were both professors. His house was always spookily silent.

"They're going through a lot with the split and Dad being away," Jan said. Melanie could be a brat. But what did Adam know about being a fifteen-year-old girl? Or a woman, for that matter? Sure, Mom cared too much about appearances. But how would he have felt if she had said his overweight mother didn't care enough?

Adam picked up Jan's hand. "I'm sorry about all that," he said. "I should have asked what was up with your mom and dad." Jan nodded. It was good to feel Adam's sympathy. He smiled sweetly and she could tell that he meant what he said. He really did care about her.

———

Back in her room, Jan breathed a sigh of relief as Adam pulled her toward him and kissed her neck and ear. They had walked quickly back from D'Angelo's, the feeling she had at the end of lunch increasing with every step. She did care about him, and he cared about her. This was what had always mattered.

Jan's bed was carefully made up with a set of matching furry white pillows her mother had gotten her online as one of her going-away gifts. Eliza's bed had a large, messy red blanket that said *Montana* across it. Against her pillow, she had a large stuffed bear that looked like it was made with real bear fur. "Guess which one's mine," Jan laughed. Adam guided her toward the bed.

"I'll take anyplace with a soft landing," he said, and Jan smiled. This was the real Adam, she told herself.

———

The rest of the weekend felt natural, as long as Jan avoided the issue of money. They took a walk around campus, saw a movie, and ate pizza at a place on Wickenden. On the way back from the pizza place, Jan bought a six-pack at the Portuguese grocery where no one ever got carded, and Andy joined them in Jan's room for an hour or so, listening to music.

To avoid any awkwardness, Jan offered to buy the pizza and paid for her own movie ticket. Adam wouldn't let her pay for the whole pizza and chipped in, Jan noticed, exactly half the check, even dividing the amount of the tip to the *penny*. Jan had a monthly allowance that her father deposited directly into her bank account. She knew if she overspent that either of her parents would cover her, no questions asked, as long as the amount wasn't huge. Not everyone's parents were as understanding as hers, Jan told herself, although the image of Adam counting out his change still grated on her.

———

Adam left early Sunday afternoon, and afterward Jan settled in, determined to get a head start on her reading for the week. Although the visit with Adam had been strained at times, it had been sad to see him sitting on the bus. He'd waved at her and she blew him a kiss. He had smiled sweetly, although she instantly regretted the gesture. It was like something a girl would do in a movie, like she was copying a cliché script.

Jan had just started on her Early Romantics assignment when Eliza barged in with a tall, thin boy and a chunkier dark-haired guy.

"Oh, hey," said Eliza. "No more love nest?" Then she turned to the boys, gesturing toward Jan. "My roomie here is a love junkie. Girl ousted me an entire forty-eight hours! You tell me, are looks deceiving or what?"

Jan shook her head and felt her face flush. The tall, good-looking guy was the one Andy had told her about from class, she was certain of that. Both of the boys looked older, and here they were in the freshman dorm with Eliza. Only her roommate could pull that off. Jan fought back a wave of embarrassment. She was tired of being so wishy-washy, tired of letting Eliza dominate her, fed up with herself for not speaking her mind more firmly when Adam criticized her family.

"It wasn't like that, Eliza and you know it!" she said. "My boyfriend from home was visiting. He's at school in Boston," she said to the boys. The tall guy hardly glanced her way, but the shorter one shook his head sympathetically, as if to say he knew all about Eliza.

"Just messing with you," Eliza said. "Don't get huffy. I tell everyone you're the best roomie a girl could have. Neat as a pin, bright as a penny."

Eliza began looking through her desk drawers, then turned to the closet. "Just got to locate my stash, then we'll be out of your way." She leaned into her closet and pulled a plastic bag from a long, plaid coat and handed it to the tall guy.

"Not a problem," Jan said. She feigned interest in her iPad, clicking to add a comment to the essay she had barely begun reading. Eliza's use of the word *penny* distracted her.

"Just one more sec," Eliza said to the guys. "Oh, my bad, I'm such a rudie—Carl, Roberto, this is Jan. She's from Manhattan, fancy—like you all. And she's *not* a slut. I was just breaking her balls. She's practically a married fucking woman."

Jan sighed. "I'm hardly that," she said with unintentional seriousness.

"Oh, really?" Eliza asked, suddenly interested. "Has the shine come off the apple?"

Jan looked at Eliza, perplexed. "The shine come off the who?" she asked, and the boys broke into gales of laughter. She realized that the guys, at least, were very stoned. Jan smiled. Although Jan was clearly on the outside of their little group, she had held her own with Eliza for once.

"Ok, chickadee," Eliza said, her hand on the door, "I'm going to get my stuff from Abby and Carl's place," she said, gesturing at the tall guy. She'd heard Eliza mention Abby before and assumed she was the tall girl with the red dreads. Jan felt a pang of envy at Eliza's effortless cool—already on sleepover terms with sophomores and juniors. "You around for dinner?" Eliza asked, as though she and Jan always shared intimate secrets at the end of the day. "I gotta have the goods."

"Sure," Jan said, not unhappy at the prospect of having someone to talk to. "Not much to tell, though. He just seemed weirdly focused on money."

"Well," Eliza said, "I can tell from experience, that's called being broke. You have to focus on this little, tiny bit that you have." Eliza squinted, as though staring into a microscope.

"I guess," Jan said, suddenly self-conscious. It was unlike her to talk openly about Adam with Eliza, never mind the fact that the two boys still stood there, listening with a stoned attentiveness. "He's just all about splitting everything down the middle. I mean down to the *cent*," Jan said.

Eliza paused and cocked her head. She looked clear-eyed, while Carl's and Roberto's eyes were glazed over. Jan wondered whether Eliza was even high. She was being unusually chatty, but seemed lucid. "Well, even my daddy, who is Mr. Stone-Cold Cheap, doesn't carry pennies in his pocket," Eliza said. "If your man is getting you down to the cent column, I say you're looking weird in the face." Eliza shook her head. "I know about weird," she said. "My family crawls with it."

Jan closed her eyes as Eliza shut the door. On the one hand, she was glad Eliza wasn't angry with her about the sexiling. In fact, Jan's demanding the room for the weekend seemed to put them on more equal footing. Still, she wasn't sure she was being fair about Adam. A few hours before, Jan had shared this very bed with him. He had held her tight and stroked her hair. What did it mean that she had been so quick to talk him down?

6

"It's the kind of party where everyone is going to have a costume. You can't get in without one. It's ten bucks apiece and a costume," Melanie said. Gerald was stuffing his face with chocolate chip cookies and swigging milk right from the container, but it was hard to object since they were in his house. Melanie twirled on the shiny metal barstool in the center of the expansive kitchen, from which she could see to the street below on both sides of the glass-encased living room. Gerald had the best house. It sucked for him that his dad had died, but at least he'd left them a sweet place to live.

"I hate dressing up," Jess said. "I vote for the least dressing up possible." Jess was also chowing down on cookies, but Melanie tried to restrain herself. Her skin looked like crap, and she couldn't deal with another morning waking up bloated, with her face a broken-out mess.

"We could do something completely unimaginative just to

get in, like vampires or witches. Dress in black, buy teeth. Done," Melanie said. Melanie continued to twirl on the barstool, getting herself dizzy. Outside, you could see people walking around with umbrellas, heads ducked down, trotting across the street. The rain made people seem all the same. Everyone hurried to get out of the cold wet. Everyone had the same cheap, black umbrella. Each time Melanie twirled around and looked out the window, the scene seemed the same. Then, something caught her eye. They were on the sixth floor, high enough not to be seen, but low enough to make out people's faces. "There's your brother," Melanie said. "Edward. Look at how he crosses the street." Melanie giggled. "He's like Mr. Unaffected-by-the-Elements." Gerald's brother, Edward, was seventeen, a track star and a senior at Rose Dyer. It was a Saturday afternoon and Edward was on his way back from a meet, waiting to cross Sixth Avenue with his Windbreaker over one shoulder, still wearing his red and blue track shorts.

"Is my mom with him?" Gerald asked, glancing out the window. "Nope. That's good."

"Why do you have such a thing about us never being here if your mom is here?" Melanie asked.

"I don't know," Gerald said. "She's kind of a neat freak. Look around. Do you see any dirt? Crumbs? Dust? Nada, right? Because she has a Dustbuster attached to her arm. It's scary." Gerald put the milk and the package of cookies away and cleared off the shiny black countertop with the back of his hand. "I just prefer the atmosphere around here without the constant whir of a vacuum."

Jess laughed. "That's like Rick. His entire purpose for living is to be sure his environment is dirt-free. Clutter is the ultimate enemy. It's like he sees a pack of gum, a hairbrush, or anything random left anywhere and he's practically in tears. Anyway, who knows, maybe we'll be the same way once we actually have to buy our own stuff, and clean it ourselves."

"Not me," Melanie said. "I'm totally at peace with dirt. What I'm not at peace with is freaking Halloween. I really cannot go to any James Jamison party wearing vampire teeth or blood on my face. It's too disgustingly lame. We have to keep thinking."

"Hey, kids." Edward walked in soaking wet, took off his sneakers in the front hall, and tossed his wet jacket onto the stool next to Melanie.

"Ah, Edward, you're getting me soaked," Melanie complained.

"Sorry," Edward said, "but you're kind of in my kitchen, on my barstool. Anyway, what are you guys doing? You should come over to RD with me after I change, and watch the girls' volleyball game. They start at four. Our girls are smokin'." Edward got a glass of water from the tap, drank it, and filled the glass again. Edward's on-again-off-again girlfriend, Ellen, was a star volleyball player. She was at least six feet tall, with long brown hair and freckles so close together she was more covered than not. Melanie could never decide if Ellen was actually pretty. If Edward thought she was, which he apparently did, she must have something going for her.

"Maybe," Melanie said, answering for the rest of them. "But we need to get costumes first. We're going to a Halloween party and it's costumes required. That's what Erika said." Gerald drew his finger across his throat in an effort to get Melanie to stop talking in front of Edward, but she didn't take the hint.

"I know!" Jess said. "Why don't we do a fifties thing. We could do *Grease*—rolled-up pants, little sweater. You could be Sandy, Melanie. Super easy."

"Maybe," Melanie said, musing. "Would I be the before-Sandy or the after-Sandy?" It was the sort of thing Melanie would say in front of Gerald and not give it a second thought, but with Edward, she was wary. He could think she was flirting with him. Edward was part of a big stoner crowd his sophomore year, but then he went away for the summer to someplace like Colorado or Wyoming, to one of those wilderness camping and hiking survival places. When he came back, he cut his hair short and started running track, which he turned out to be great at. He wasn't as cute now, in Melanie's opinion, but he was broad-shouldered, with a trim runner's waist, and he had slightly droopy blue eyes. She liked his smile, which was a little crooked.

"Sounds like the typical teen Slutoween," Edward said. "But knock yourselves out." With that, Edward took a box of cereal, disappeared down the hall to his room, and shut the door. It was deflating to have Edward call them slutty, but then again, it was a pretty easy costume to pull off, and Melanie already owned a pair of shiny black leggings from American Apparel. In fact, everything they needed could be had at AA, except maybe some fake eyelashes.

"All right. Done," Melanie said. "Who cares what *he* thinks," she said, nodding in the direction of Edward's room. "What am

I going to do, go to a party with a sheet over my head? Gerald, what are you wearing? We've got to leave and get whatever we need. I have eight tons of homework due Monday, and my mom is making me go with her and Erika tonight to this movie about India that her friend made. It's ridiculous. My mom writes for magazines that sell all this shit made by these people in India, where their factories are always falling down on top of them, and then she goes dragging me off to these depressing movies about how all of our clothes are made by small children sitting chained to the floor. It's like, have your own guilt."

Jess laughed. "Try having four gay parents and then we can talk about guilt. I am never, ever saying the word *gender* in the front of my kids, if I even have any."

"Maybe I'll just suit up in my old football stuff," Gerald said. "I can wear the jersey from the Downtown League, pads— maybe I can even fit into the pants." Gerald seemed depressed since Edward arrived, as though Edward, even once he had left the room, were watching over him.

"That's not exactly inspired, Gerald," Jess said. "Can't you at least be what's-his-face?"

"Seriously?" Melanie said. "No way am I walking in as Sandy with Gerald as what's-his-face, Danny. Just do the football player thing." Gerald cast a momentary hurt glance at Melanie, which Melanie chose to ignore. She hated when Gerald made that injured-puppy face at her.

Gerald tied his sneakers as Jess and Melanie picked out the right leotard for Melanie's Sandy on Jess's phone. "I don't think it's really as slutty as Edward says. People wear bunny tails, and almost nothing else. Edward is the biggest stomper of people's grooves." Melanie sniffed.

"Don't get your panties in a knot," Edward said, coming up behind Melanie with his heavy track sweatshirt on. "I make no judgment. You liberated bitches can expose all the T and A you please. You won't get any complaints from me." Edward smiled with exaggerated lasciviousness at Melanie, who flushed. Then she frowned at Gerald, who clearly must have seen his brother come down the hall, but still let Melanie go off about him. "Thanks," Melanie mouthed at Gerald. Gerald looked moodily away. He seemed to get annoyed whenever the attention turned to Edward.

No one said anything in the elevator on the way down to the street, and then a lady got on with a stroller on the fourth floor, and Edward offered to get out and take the stairs. "Bye, kids," he said. "Come to the game if you can. Ellen is getting scouted by Princeton. Should be a hot game."

"Sure." Gerald waved lamely. "She's scouted by Princeton and he's applying early action to Yale. Kind of makes me sick."

"I know. I hate perfect people. And I'm practically surrounded by them," Melanie said.

"You guys should try being only children. The only child of four parents. At least someone is already perfect in your family, so your parents can lay off you. I'm their only hope. You should have seen my moms when I told them they were dropping me to the slow math class. It was like I killed babies." Jess opened her umbrella, although the rain had slowed to a drizzle. "Come on under, Melanie," she said. "Your hair is more important than any part of Gerald."

"Of course it is," Melanie said, and she joined arms with Jess and let Gerald walk along next to them down Sixth Avenue, hands shoved into the pockets of his baggy jeans.

"You know for sure we can even get into this thing, after going through all this trouble?" Gerald asked. He had to shout to be heard over the rain and traffic.

"Sure. Easy-breezy," Melanie said without looking in Gerald's direction. Erika had invited Melanie to the party because their mother suggested it. Mom had a thing about them going out together on Halloween and New Year's, nights when it was easier for her if they kept track of each other. Erika had checked with Binky and she'd said it was fine—the more girls the better, was what Chris Primrose had said. But Melanie hadn't asked about Gerald. She didn't care one way or the other if Gerald came to the party, but now she had invited him, she was stuck. She'd have to make sure Erika got him in. Primrose was a junior jock, and Gerald would be too intimidated to ask him himself. That was the most annoying thing about Gerald. Really about all her friends: how everything fun or worth doing always seemed to be up to her.

7

Erika was grateful for the salad bar at Rose Dyer. There were always two kinds of everything—two kinds of lettuce, two kinds of dressing, two choices of beans, even two kinds of tomato: sliced, and the little round cherry tomatoes. It made being a vegetarian at school almost simpler than being one at home. The only problem was the chicken.

It hadn't been difficult to give up beef, because cows were attractively large-eyed. They seemed docile and forgiving when they huddled in those mud-filled fields and endured all kinds of terrible weather in their silent, steaming masses.

Chickens were different. She found their feet particularly repulsive, almost evil-seeming. She really didn't care if chickens were wiped off the face of the earth tomorrow. But she liked to eat chicken, especially chicken salad. Several times since she had become a vegetarian she'd been tempted to place a heaping serving of the cafeteria curry chicken salad on her tray. Who'd notice? Who'd care? It was only her own conscience that kept her from doing it. Erika had an especially zealous conscience. This had been true even in preschool, when it had been common for kids to try to sneak extra cookies from the tray at snack time. Even other kids' crimes gave Erika a slight pang in her stomach, a chill, a dizziness. No, she was incapable of eating chicken at this point. She'd made a rule for herself and she was stuck with it.

"Hey, rabbit. Nice eats." Morris was giving her a hard time yet again about her lunch. She didn't know why he didn't go off-campus for lunch, like most people. Erika liked the cafeteria food, but most kids would rather eat bagels from the bodega than eat from the salad bar, like she did, or from the hot lunch counter, like Morris. It was part of Morris's geekiness that he ate at school.

"Rabbits don't eat legumes. Beans are legumes. Rabbits eat cabbages and roots." Erika took her water bottle off her tray and sat down across from Morris.

"Okay, then, rat. Rats eat everything."

Erika narrowed her eyes at Morris. Of course, being called *rat* by anyone else would be an insult, but Erika liked rats, and she knew Morris did too. "I think they eat meat, Morris, they're scavengers, not herbivores."

"Oh, yeah. Got to work on that. So what's up with this Halloween thing Binky's talking about?"

Erika motioned that she had to finish chewing. Really, she hesitated because she worried Morris was going to refuse to go, because the party was uptown. She had to make sure she put the idea in the best possible light. "Well, Binky said it's in this amazing townhouse. James Jamison, who knows Chris and Binky from when they went to school up there, is having it. Binky says the house has a screening room, with a full-sized movie screen that rolls down from the ceiling. It's all glass and there are like twenty rooms."

Morris rolled his eyes. "You're telling me I have to go to some preppy costume party? Upper White Side style? And the dude has a double name—James Jamison? That is like the pink pants of names. Damn, does your friend Binky have some poor taste in the male of the species. That girl needs some sort of brain surgery to excise that douchebag-seeking section of the cerebrum."

Erika laughed. It was a relief that Morris disapproved of Christopher Primrose, since she wasn't too certain about Chris either, but she felt loyal to Binky. "I thought your philosophy was live and let live, Morris? Do you think Binky or I would judge you for going out with someone who . . ."

"Someone who what, girl?" Morris raised his eyebrows. "I'm waiting. . . ."

"You know," Erika said, blushing. "A girl who wasn't serious . . ." Erika trailed off, losing conviction under the heat of Morris's stare.

"You can't even say it because the girl version of Chris-the-Playa Primrose doesn't exist. Oh, they pretend to. Girls like Lani Elliot, who are all guess-who-I-did-last-night? But then I'm like, who cares? I am like, bring that shit on. See, that's where the species is different. We want to get it on, and move on. You ladies do not want that. Sad thing about that girl Lani is she's all busy showing a dog how to be a dog, and he don't care." Morris shook his head dismissively.

"I don't see how you can tell what a girl actually wants if you haven't asked her," Erika said. She was no fan of Lani Elliot and her crowd, but it annoyed her that Morris was speaking for all girls. There was more than one way to be unusual. But Morris wasn't done.

"You ladies, well, maybe not you in particular, Erika, but ladies do get their freak on, sure. But, like Foss says, and he grew up down South so he's got the flavor, a good bitch knows when to bite." Morris dug into his gray-looking cafeteria burger.

Erika looked at Morris in wonder. "Why are we talking about Lani Elliot?" she asked. "What does any of this have to do with going uptown for Halloween?"

Morris grinned. "It's a known fact that white guys who are douches to women are assholes to the black man."

"Morris," Erika said. "We can always leave. I don't really care, but Binky does, so I think we should all go. Besides, you don't have any actual evidence that this is a racist party." Erika hated when Morris got illogical.

Erika was done eating, but Morris was now working his way through his bag of chips, eating noisily as he considered what Erika said. He grew suddenly serious.

"You need some experience, girl. You have basically none."

Morris nodded and picked up another chip. He pointed the chip at her. "You white people are just so ignorant."

"That really hurts, Morris. All these generalizations . . ." Erika paused, confused. "I don't know. Maybe they're true, but they make me so frustrated." The therapist Erika had gone to in middle school had encouraged Erika to assert her boundaries. Morris had definitely crossed hers, but she struggled to explain how.

"I know, girl. I'm sorry," Morris said. "I'll stop." Morris held up his hands and did a quick little bow. But then he continued. "I got an idea about what to wear to this Klan gathering. I'm thinking 'hear no evil.' But ghetto. Shave my head, wear those big ol' headphones Foss has. Good idea, huh? I'll listen to my tunes, don't have to talk to any coked-up Dalton boys. Only problem then is who's keeping an eye on you girls." He frowned. "You girls are a lot of trouble. You telling me I'm going to have to keep track of both you and Binky at this party?"

"I don't even drink, Morris. What trouble am I?" Erika was annoyed again. She took good care of herself. Even her mother trusted her absolutely.

———

After lunch with Morris, Erika had study hall, and then math. Usually, she enjoyed last-period math. She liked Martin, the math teacher, and how his name fit his personality perfectly, and how he wore brown jackets, brown socks, and brown shoes. His entire appearance was consistent with the name Martin, and there were few people you could say this about. Even his wife was Martin-ish, Erika knew, because she had met her at the end-of-the-year potluck last spring. She wore her brown hair tucked behind her ears, and she wore worn-down loafers, which were also brown.

Erika stared out the window at the garden courtyard. Someone's mom was down there planting bulbs. Her own mother never volunteered at school, although she sometimes donated beautiful clothes she got from magazine editors to the school's yearly auctions and rummage sales. Erika was proud of her mother on those rare occasions when she came to school for meetings and conferences.

Her mother always looked put together, and she wore pretty shoes—sandals, pumps, or trim little boots. She liked that her mother still had long hair, and that it was silky to the touch. Her mother looked, especially now, since Dad left, like a woman in a magazine, like someone with expectations, secrets, and plans— with maybe more mystery than you actually wanted in a mom.

Erika tried to redirect her thoughts back to Martin, to the unslippery reality of mathematics. Math, Erika felt, was like an amazingly complex game that grew in complexity with understanding. It was essential not to miss anything. With people, Erika had discovered, things were far easier if you skipped over big parts of what they said and did.

Her phone buzzed under her desk and she glanced down at the screen. It was Melanie. "Wait 4 me out front," it said. It was unusual for Melanie to text Erika. The question of what Melanie might want distracted Erika for the remainder of math.

After class, Erika met Binky in the main lobby, where they

always met on Thursdays to study for their Friday French quizzes. "Come outside with me to meet Mel. She has to tell me something," Erika said. Outside, Melanie was standing by a cluster of dirty-looking benches no one ever sat on. She was standing with Jess and Gerald. It was horribly windy and all three of them had hoodies pulled up. Melanie had her haughty look on, eyebrows raised, cheeks sucked in. "What's going on?" Erika asked.

"Ask," Melanie commanded Gerald.

"Oh, yeah," Gerald said, noncommittally. "Just wondering about that party. Whether I could come too?" Erika looked at Binky, but Binky had suddenly dashed off and grabbed Chris Primrose and was dragging him over.

"Ask *him*," insisted Binky in her husky voice.

"Ask him what?" Primrose asked. Gerald blushed a deep red, and Erika felt sorry for him. She didn't know why Melanie was making such a production of the thing, if she was the one who invited Gerald in the first place.

"Oh, these guys said there was a party uptown," Gerald trailed off.

"Yeah," Primrose said. "Guy told me I could bring as many friends as I wanted, as long as they didn't have dicks." He laughed. "So, I guess that's your call, dude." None of the girls laughed or said anything, and Binky punched Chris hard on the shoulder. Primrose cast an angry look at Binky, but then his face softened.

"Just messing with you dude," Primrose said. "You can

come, man, so long as it's only you and the ladies. No moochers or tagalongs. Ten bucks apiece." Then Chris grabbed Binky by the hand and dragged her away. Gerald shot Melanie a look of relief, but she was already walking away, arm in arm with Jess, leaving Erika and Gerald together in an awkward silence.

"It's better than sitting home," said Erika kindly.

"Yeah," Gerald said, gazing after Melanie and Jess. "Too bad only assholes ever have good parties." Then he took his phone out of his pocket, bringing the conversation to an end.

Erika walked alone back into the building. She figured sooner or later Binky would show up in the library to study. She sat down at a table by the window, and was surprised to see Gerald still out front, sitting on one of the abandoned-looking benches staring down at his phone. Melanie, Erika thought, had been needlessly cruel to Gerald, the way she sometimes was to her. But Gerald had acted like it had been only Primrose who'd insulted him, like in his eyes her sister could do no wrong.

8

Gerald had been in beautiful apartments before. But this wasn't an apartment. An apartment had a beginning and an end. You could find someone you were looking for in a New York City apartment. Gerald had been looking for Melanie Russell for so long now, he'd grown doubtful of ever finding her. There were too many rooms, and every room he entered was smoke-filled and crowded wall-to-wall with teenagers in costumes. There was one room that held three nuns, all of them blond, all of them identically habited in nun hats, whatever those things were called, and loose-fitting white blouses. None of the nun girls wore anything on the bottom but black bikini bottoms with stockings and black heels. In another room, there was a scarecrow of indeterminate gender, and a tree, which was clearly female, busty, and clad mainly in leaves. There were several rubber-faced president zombies and a lone banker clad in enormous, cardboard hundred-dollar bills.

But nowhere could he find Sandy and Rizzo.

Gerald recalled that when they'd first arrived Melanie had asked him to get her a drink, which he had. There was a keg of beer in the kitchen, along with a mysterious pink-colored punch, and he had chosen the punch. That was before he'd taken the joint someone had passed him, before he drank his own glass or two of punch, or had it been more? He was having difficulty remembering how many drinks he might have consumed. He seemed to remember entering and leaving the kitchen numerous times. One time, he'd nearly knocked over a kitchen chair, and a guy with short black hair and a stubby mustache had grabbed hold of it and said "Whoa, fella," as he'd stumbled past. He thought, but then dismissed the thought, that the guy had been dressed as Hitler. But then again, maybe they did that on the Upper East Side. He'd only been there to go to museums. Who knew what might pass for humor? His brother had been scornful when he'd told him about the party. Edward knew about such things. He'd even gone, for middle school, to a selective public school in the neighborhood Gerald was now in. His brother had told him, when he left their Chelsea apartment, to "watch his back." Edward didn't usually pay all that much attention to him, and in the moment, it had felt satisfying, in a masculine way, to be advised by his brother.

Each time Gerald entered the Jamisons' immaculate pale-green and white tiled kitchen, he had seen Morris and Erika. Erika had said to him, "Come find us here when you guys are ready to go. I'm afraid to go out there! There's like two hundred people here!" Gerald thought there were probably more than two hundred people. It was hard to say, because every room he went into was filled with bodies—smoking, drinking, groping teenage bodies. He'd been in so many rooms he'd lost count. One room held a pool table, and another held a large screen and two rows of plush chairs, but what was the room for that was mostly empty, containing only a single enormous mirror, a thick wooden bar pressed against it, and a small metal contraption on a blue mat? Why would anyone have an entire room for so few things?

Then, finally, he saw her. It was in the room in which the music was loudest. The song that was playing had been a hit over the summer. It had a crazy thwanking beat, and half of it was in another language, maybe Korean or Japanese. The girls were all dancing like the girls danced in the video that went with the song. They shimmied while bending over each knee, right, left, right. Mel was dancing like that, but not bending all the way over, really only hinting at doing the dance. She was no longer with Jess. She looked so unlike herself at first he had to force himself to cross the room to her. The shirt she was wearing hung off her slender shoulders and exposed a glorious expanse of pale, unblemished skin. Even her slight shimmying produced a vision Gerald could neither turn from nor entirely take in. Her hair tumbled across her shoulders and down her back. Was she always that blond, or had she done something to her hair? Was the blondness part of the costume? Her lips were full and pouty. She was standing more than dancing, but still with a slight shimmy. She was just opening her lips to laugh at something someone was saying.

The someone was tall. One of the guys who'd been downstairs taking people's coats when they'd arrived. Perhaps this was James Jamison himself, billionaire boy. Gerald loathed him the moment he laid eyes on him. He loathed the way his straight brown hair flopped over one eye, the way he stood there in his round-sleeved pirate's shirt, eye-patch on top of his head, somehow in costume and not looking like an asshole.

It was hard to get across the fucking room with his shoulder pads on. Other guys kept grabbing him by the pads and shaking him like he was some kind of rag doll. Occasionally, a guy threw his arms forward locked in a block that Gerald involuntarily bounced away from. He knew they were laughing at him and that he was drunk, but he thought if he could only cross the room, arrive at Melanie's side, his dizziness would subside and he would be having fun like the rest of them. They'd stop laughing if they knew who he was with. He saw a few kids from school, passed Jess, and raised his glass to her to say hello, but she turned her head at the wrong moment. When he looked away from Jess, back to where Melanie stood, she was gone.

Girls did not simply vanish, Gerald knew, so she must have left the room through a back hallway he had not yet arrived at. He pushed on through the crowd. "Hey, dude, whatever team you're on, you're losing!" some wise guy called. Gerald stumbled. It wasn't because he was that drunk. It was just crowded and the carpets were thick. The shimmy-dance song finally ended and a

Thongs' song came on. "Shit, not these homos," he heard some-one say. He wondered if that was true, were the Thongs, with their skinny jeans and high-tops, gay? It would serve the girls right. All those screaming girls.

The hallway that led from the rear of the room was wider than Gerald expected. There was an alcove in the middle of it, and a balcony beyond that. A wall of windows led up to the balcony, and the lights of the city shone through them, mak-ing Gerald certain of his own slowly returning sobriety. There was the city. An alley, another townhouse next door. A garden with a few scraggly tomato plants. A terrace on which sat seven or eight elaborately carved jack-o'-lanterns, still lit, still glow-ing. These objects were all clear and nameable. He was not so very drunk.

Suddenly, the door to the balcony slammed open, and a high-heeled shoe appeared, then a well-formed, spandex-clad calf. A girl tumbled in. A blond girl, still stumbling. It was Mel-anie, and she needed help. Gerald shot forward. He was fine now, and she needed him. There was someone still out there on the balcony. That asshole from before, that pirate asshole. Melanie was running from him, right into his arms.

"Oh, Gerald . . . it's just you," Melanie murmured. She looked startled, as if she had just awakened from a dream. Her eyes seemed too large for her face, and her lipstick was smudged across her cheek. She grabbed onto his arm. He could scarcely understand what she was saying. Her top had stretched out and now one shoulder was completely exposed. Holding her the way he did, he could look down, and just barely make out the outline of her nipple.

The room at the end of the hall was a perfect little room. A light was on and the door was open, but no one, miraculously, was in there. There was a small leather couch and a white fur rug. The rug had a head on it with teeth and ears. It was an actual bear rug. Somehow, he and Melanie were both on the rug. She had wanted to feel it. She had needed to lie down a moment. He'd gotten down there with her, and now it was so easy to see all the way down her top, to where the almost transparent material of her bra had slipped. He still felt the urge to help her, knew she needed him, but that urge was mingled with something else, a stronger urge to reach out, to touch her breast. Then suddenly, she was kissing him, and everything he wanted was possible. He felt the irresistible urge to press his mouth on her nipple. When he did, Melanie let out a little gasp, a moan. She was reaching up his shirt. It was an astonishing turn of events. She was drunk, he knew that. But she wanted him, the same way he had always wanted her. He felt her between her legs. She was moving herself closer to him. She was kissing him hard. Somehow, he threw off his shirt. His shoulder pads got in the way, and for a moment he was caught up, his shirt snagged, but somehow he got rid of the cumbersome pads. She twisted underneath him, making her girl sounds. There was the moment, just as he climbed on top of her, feeling her hip bones sharp against him, when he heard her say something, something he knew he needed to hear. He opened his eyes and looked at her. Her face was contorted, with lipstick hopelessly everywhere. She was still making her little mewing sounds. Then, it was as if someone pressed fast-forward on a movie. He thrust himself into her. For a moment, he felt for sure he was in a dream. It wasn't the first such dream he'd had. Then it was over.

When he looked down at Melanie's face, she was no longer staring up at him, and she was no longer making any sounds. She had passed out.

———

"Hey, Binky, that little blondie girl you all brought here is so fucked up. You got to get her out. I took her out onto the balcony because I was afraid she was going to lose it on my mom's rug, and she started grabbing me, trying to kiss me and shit."

"Melanie's drunk?" Erika looked up from her cards. She, Morris, Binky, and Christopher Primrose had been sitting in the kitchen for most of the party, playing cards. Something had changed. Christopher was no longer shepherding Binky around, moving her to dark corners of the room. He was sitting next to her, hand on her knee, as if they were going out. Erika had been transfixed by that change the entire night, contemplating what it might mean if Binky were now Christopher Primrose's girlfriend. She had almost completely forgotten about Melanie and Jess.

"Shit. Where is she? Where's the other one?" Morris got up, his enormous headphones resting behind his protruding ears, and began following James Jamison in his pirate costume back to the balcony.

"I guess she freaked when I told her to get off of me, and she came back inside. I thought she went this way. . . ." James led Erika, Binky, Christopher, and Morris down the windowed hallway, past the burning jack-o'-lanterns, the stunning cityscape. James walked stiffly, full of concern, evidently eager to rid himself of responsibility for the drunk Melanie. "She must be passed out somewhere."

"Oh my God, my mother's going to kill me," Erika said.

"Not your fault." Morris tried to shut her down.

"I should have at least watched out for her. We were supposed to watch out for each other. Mom kept telling Melanie she should check in on me during the party. She forgot to remind me to check on Melanie."

Morris shook his head. "Your mom is great, but she has this weird idea Melanie is about eighteen years old and you're about ten." Erika smiled. But she understood why her mom thought like that. Melanie was tough. She was the sort of person you didn't think needed looking after.

Then suddenly James raised his hand for them to stop, his cardboard-cutout hook still attached at the wrist. Someone was retching loudly in the bathroom off the hallway, and James opened the door slightly. It was Gerald. He was shirtless and he was kneeling over the toilet. Just above his head was a little row of the prettiest hand towels Erika had ever seen. They were off-white and had tiny yellow and green daffodils stitched on them.

"That's one of ours," Morris said. "I feel so proud."

James shut the door and raised his eyebrows meaningfully.

"One down, two to go."

When James opened the door at the end of the hall, though, he blocked the doorway. Then he shut it again quickly behind him. "Hey, buddy, let's let the girls deal with that, all right?— we'll get bathroom boy cleaned up."

Melanie lay on a white bear rug in the middle of the wood-paneled, book-lined room, with Jess kneeling over her, her back to the door. Erika could see Melanie's bare calf, her black patent leather heels, a strand of blond curls. Jess turned around when Erika and Binky came into the room. "I found her like this," she said.

Erika's first thought was: *Is my sister alive?*

————

Erika let Jess pull Melanie's panties back up, and her black Lycra leggings. Erika lifted Melanie's butt off the floor, and supported her upper body, while Jess did the pulling. Melanie's hair fell across Erika's face. The bump-it in her hair, which had been the cause of hilarity earlier in the evening, had come loose and banged Erika across the forehead. Erika felt a surge of nausea. Erika was not, as her mother often explained to relatives, a hugger. The smell of another human body so close to her, the press of skin against skin, had always produced in her a nervous reaction. She could see why it would be soothing to lose oneself in the feel of another's touch, but she had never had that experience. The one possible exception was her mother. With her mother, Erika liked to be close enough to lean into her on the couch or in the kitchen when she was cooking dinner. Mom called it "the Erika," this leaning in, as if it were a dance move.

But this closeness to Melanie was not that kind of closeness. This was more like being a nurse, moving her sister's body from one position to another. Oddly, it was only once she envisioned herself that way, as a sort of medical professional, a person who should be in uniform, a white jacket, rather than in a Halloween costume with a fluttering black silk veil over her head, her version of "see no evil," that it occurred to Erika that her sister had been raped. The shock of finding Melanie drunk, lying helplessly on the floor, had somehow registered first as catastrophe enough.

"We have to call 911," Erika said. "I have to call my mom. . . ."

"I don't know," Jess said. "I think we ought to wake her up. Maybe it's not what we think." Jess was leaning over Melanie, nudging her, calling softly, "Melanie, Melanie," as if she were just waking her up from a particularly sound sleep.

Erika jabbed Melanie hard between the ribs. "You've got to really whack Mel to get her up. She's the soundest sleeper in the family." Erika jabbed Melanie again, then a third time. Finally, Melanie opened her eyes. Her blue eyes were red and squinty. She saw where she was and sighed and put her head back down. "Mel, Mel, we're here, talk to us," Erika said. Melanie groaned and turned away. She curled her shoulder forward, as if she were in her own bed and could roll over and go back to sleep. "Mel, you can't sleep here, you hear me? You've got to get up or they're going to call the police." Something in Melanie was roused at that, and she came to with surprising quickness. She sat up and looked around and seemed to recall something vaguely unpleasant. "Fuck," she said. "Fuck, Jess, fuck . . . that punch was so strong . . . and then someone passed me a joint." Melanie paused then, and looked around. "And we came in here and then . . ." She put her head in her hands. "The two of you found me? Just you two?"

"Yeah," Jess lied before Erika could open her mouth.

"Good," she said. She smiled faintly at Jess. Then she looked at Erika, her eyes steady but bloodshot. She raised her finger and pointed at her sister. "If you tell Mom about this, I'll fucking kill you." She spoke steadily, emphasizing both *fucking* and *kill*. There was something about Melanie's look that made Erika feel the threat was not an overstatement. Erika recoiled. Melanie's breath was foul with the smell of stale alcohol. Her heart skipped a beat. It was not a secret she could keep, but she couldn't tell it either. What did people do in such situations, she wondered, and she wished, not for the first time, that the truth could be conveyed in some way other than in words.

"Let's get you home," Jess said softly, still kneeling in her black Rizzo capris. "We'll find the guys and go."

"Let them get their own way home," Melanie said. "The thought of Gerald makes me want to puke."

9

Jan hated Halloween, but would have felt like a loser if she wasn't doing something that weekend. Fortunately, Adam was visiting and Andy had heard of the perfect party, an "uncostume" party off-campus. The uncostume party was down near Fox Point, a corner of the east side of Providence that remained heavily immigrant and was somewhat low-income. It was the perfect place for a Halloween party. The Portuguese families in the neighborhood all had the groove, with lots of little kids in Batman and princess costumes roaming around. The drug dealers who stood on the corner of Wickenden and dealt to Bostonians who used the convenience of Interstate 175 to score their weed and coke were in scant evidence. Police presence was too much for them on Halloween night.

Andy, Adam, and Jan stopped in at the tiny storefront wine shop on Sheldon Street, just before heading into the less affluent part of the neighborhood. "Here's the place, if we want wine to bring," Jan said. "The other liquor stores down there are only going to have Cold Duck."

"All right. How much are we getting, ladies?" Adam had his ID, which was pretty flawless as such things go. He stopped in front of the door of the liquor store and stuck his hands in his pockets. It was just what Jan was afraid of.

"We should probably get two bottles," Jan said, and handed Adam forty dollars. Thankfully, Andy didn't seem notice, or she didn't seem to care, that Adam wasn't paying for the wine.

"Cool. Andy, are you participating in this illicit purchase, or are you taking your chances on what they've got down there?" Adam had already folded the forty dollars and put it in his pocket.

"Oh," Andy said, looking at Jan and shrugging. "I guess I kind of figured Jan was covering it. Thought maybe I'd get you guys brunch or something." Andy was cool, Jan thought, letting the whole thing slide. But Adam wouldn't let up.

"Oh, we're eating in the dorm. So, you know." Adam's face betrayed no emotion. He stood there blankly, as if his insistence had no meaning, put no pressure on Jan.

"Jesus Christ, Adam, just get two bottles and don't worry about it. Andy and I are always owing each other ten or twenty. It's nothing." Jan wished she had kept control of her voice, wished she didn't feel a warm blush spread across her face.

While Adam was in the store, Jan and Andy waited outside. The wind had kicked up and it was blowing moist, cool air in from the river. "Sorry about that," Jan said with a grimace. "Not sure what it is."

"He's just funny about money. Lots of people are," Andy said.

"You don't understand, Andy, this is a thing with him." Jan spoke in hushed tones, glancing occasionally through the lightly fogged liquor-store window. There was a long line. Adam was still three or four patrons back from the wood-paneled checkout counter. "He used to be sort of careful with money. Now it's like all he thinks about. Well, not all, but it seems like it figures into everything. It's like he thinks of everything anyone does in terms of what it's *worth*."

Andy laughed. "Well, at least he's thinking about stuff. Maybe more people should think about what everything's actually worth."

"I don't think Adam is thinking about money in any deep way. It's like he doesn't know he does it."

Andy began to speak, but Jan shook her head. Adam was at the register. His face looked soft and boyish through the window as he reached into his pocket and handed over his ID. He didn't look nervous as the clerk peered at him, then at the license, then back at Adam. "Anyway, I know what you're going to say. I have to talk to him. I know."

"Yep. That you do." Jan shot Andy a warning look, as the string of bells on the liquor store door tinkled and Adam strode out with his plastic bag. He handed Jan two dollars and forty cents change and grinned broadly. "They had some seriously cheap Bulgarian merlot. I got us three bottles."

———

The crowd filled an old warehouse building that had been converted into mini lofts. The party was in two adjacent lofts and spilled out into the hallways. The invite was specific: no costumes permitted. You showed up in costume and you were automatically disinvited.

The hallways of the building were a dark gray, almost black, with high ceilings and weird flickering fluorescent lights. The crowd was mostly sophomores and juniors. Andy had been invited by a guy in her poetry workshop. It wasn't the edgy crowd that hung around the central quad, with their dreadlocks, motorcycle boots, and hipster thrift-shop sweaters—the Stainless Guy's group, as Jan had come to think of them. The music was loud enough so you had to shout to be heard at all, but Jan felt good. Adam was holding her hand and swaying to the beat of the music. The lights were dim. Both apartments had huge black sheets covering all the furniture and candles for lights, which made the whole thing feel kind of spooky and Halloweenish. Jan had on a black thrift-shop peasant skirt with a black tee and lace-up low-heeled black boots, and she was, with her asymmetrical haircut and her bangs, about as edgy as anyone else. Adam seemed to be loosening up. He was on his second or third glass of merlot. He didn't seem worried about who drank what or who'd paid what anymore. Maybe the money thing was a form of anxiety he was feeling in the first months of school. That could happen to anyone.

It was close to midnight when the guy from Andy's poetry workshop passed Jan and Adam a little orange plastic bag. It was someone's idea of party favors. In it were a few dried mushrooms that looked like the shriveled ears of a small animal—a cat or a squirrel. "A little late for that now, isn't it?" Jan said.

Jan had tried mushrooms once before. It had been in the mountains at the cabin of her high school friend Marcy, and Marcy's brother had broken the 'shrooms out one afternoon, when the parents had gone off to a barbecue with friends.

At first, she hadn't felt anything. She and Marcy had decided to take a hike on a nearby trail. They'd hiked the same trail at least once already that summer. Marcy led the way, with her long, curly blond hair pulled back in a braid. Marcy was a jock—captain of the basketball team at Rose Dyer—and she moved briskly through the woods and up the rocky trail with Jan following several paces behind. Suddenly, Jan felt the struggle to keep up with Marcy give way to a feeling of nearly limitless energy in her limbs. It was as though she were springing forward effortlessly. At the same time, the green in the woods around her had intensified. Marcy stopped suddenly in her tracks and both girls started laughing at some unspoken joke. The green was too hilariously green. The rocks too vehemently real. The clouds, foolishly mobile. The whole world had begun to exaggerate itself.

Jan remembered standing in a small clearing in the woods, watching the clouds pass overhead, and the gray-blue creek water run over the gray-blue creek stones, laughing at the unnecessary beauty, the startling particularity of things, and then running back down the wooded chaos of the path, until it was all over

and they were somehow back at the cabin. How thirsty s
been then, horribly thirsty, and with an aching behind her eyes
she felt would never go away.

And here was Adam now, a little after midnight, holding
this bag of mushrooms, looking questioningly at Jan. He didn't
want to do them, she could tell, but he was deferring to her. She
wasn't sure what to say. But it didn't seem to her like a time in
their relationship for caution.

"I guess it is Halloween and all," Adam said. "What do you
think?"

"Maybe it's something we should do. Something you and I
should do together?"

"What about Andy?" Adam asked.

"She left with that guy from her class." Jan laughed. Andy
had tapped Jan on the shoulder as she walked past her and
pointed toward the door. The guy was cute enough, but Andy
gave Jan a slight shrug of her shoulders as if to say she didn't
know what she was doing. Andy had her hot-and-heavy guy
down at Columbia, but they weren't supposed to be exclusive.

Maybe it was the wine, or maybe Adam, too, felt the relationship was in need of some crucial step, but without saying
anything more, Adam pulled out a mushroom cap and popped
it in his mouth.

———

The Silver Top diner was somewhere downtown, though Jan
was never quite sure where. They had walked there, that she
knew, but when the diner appeared, it was as if out of nowhere.

They hadn't had a destination. They'd left the party and walked west on Sheldon Street, the streets emptied of costumed children, littered with Halloween debris—toilet paper and shaving cream cans, candy wrappers, and the odd plastic toy. Adam had picked up a green and white plastic whistle on a green plastic cord and blown into it, but it had failed to produce a sound. He'd blown again and again, puffing out his cheeks, in a way that should have been funny, but which had struck Jan as symbolically futile. There was nothing sweet about those plastic toys, that landfill trash. She wished people would stop making such things, and she'd felt an actual pang in her chest at the instant realization that they would not, that the factories were permanent, wherever they were; factories now were essential to the landscape. She'd wanted to tell Adam what she was thinking, and to put the damn whistle down, but she couldn't get started. A terrible silence had begun to fill her. It was as thick as the outer dark. It was like being hungry but too ill to eat. There were terrible things that needed to be said, but the silence within her had kept swallowing them up. She couldn't even say his name. If she could have, she was sure the rest would have come tumbling out, but there'd been something acrid now in those syllables. *Adam*—no, she couldn't say it. She'd felt like crying, but tears had also been impossible, so she'd walked on, trailing him by half a step, the pathetic whistle now hanging around his neck from the plastic cord. She'd wanted to tell him it was no good, to get rid of the thing, but she'd kept quiet, and it had remained hanging there, extraneous and obscene.

They'd kept walking toward the water, then toward downtown, then along a street that no longer curved around itself in the concentricity that was Providence, and then they had arrived, mysteriously, at the Silver Top.

It was necessary, with the sun beginning to rise, and a breeze kicking up off the water, to be in the Silver Top diner with a cup of coffee and a fiesta omelet. Adam was rumpled, his eyes half closed and his lips pursed in a way Jan had never seen before. He looked at Jan across the white Formica table and took her hand. For the past hour or so of walking, she had been trapped in her silence. Each of them had been in their own sealed-off world of darkness, of the light they were heading toward. In the end, something had loosened in her, the effect of the drug perhaps wearing off, and she'd reached for him, and they'd held hands tightly. It had been terrible, and lonesome, but they had walked their way out of it. They had been like children, Jan felt, wandering alone in the dark, helpless, but ultimately good and brave.

The only other customers in the diner were a couple of truck drivers and a table of costumed party kids. One girl was a vampire. Another was wearing a pink and white cardboard box on her head, which at one point in the evening had probably been a part of a clever costume. There was a small, sharp-jawed boy with them, and a stocky boy, who nodded at her when they came in. It was Mr. Stainless's friend, Roberto.

"What I don't remember is how we got on this walking thing. Why didn't we just go hang out in the quad, or in your room?" Adam's voice was hoarse and his skin had a yellowish tint under the fluorescent diner lights. Jan needed to use the bathroom, but wasn't ready to leave the table, to confront her own reflection in the hard-edged, unforgiving solitude of the diner's ladies' room.

"Don't you remember? It was your idea to go downtown. You wanted to see the city of Providence; you asked at one point where the fucking city was." She didn't elaborate on how his question had been answered with her own silence.

Adam laughed. For an instant, it was like being home again, back in New York, with the old Adam. The old Adam laughed with his mouth turned down slightly at the corners. He seemed not to realize that Jan had been silent, brooding during their trip, that in her mind, she had destroyed everything—their past, their future, their entire relationship, negated by a toxic, hate-filled silence. The plastic whistle that had hung around his neck was gone now. For a second, she wondered if she'd imagined the whole thing, but then she noticed it on the floor beside Adam's foot, discarded as it should have been back on Sheldon Street. What if he'd never picked the stupid thing up?

"I know what I was looking for the whole time. Remember how quiet we were, how it was like we were on some unspoken quest?" Adam asked. "It wasn't the city of Providence really. I was looking for this." Jan stared hard at him. Was everything somehow suddenly, impossibly okay?

"Yeah, it's the Silver Top," Jan said. "It does feel like we were looking for it the whole time. Funny thing is, I've been here before, but can never remember how to get here."

"No, I mean, this, being with you without all the other people. Being with you not at college. I wanted to find the city because the city isn't the school." Jan thought about how the school *was* there, was everywhere in Providence. Roberto was there—he sat a few feet from them, in a booth with green vinyl seats. Jan even began to point him out to Adam, to relay the whole story of the semiotics class, the refrigerator, and Mr. Stainless. But it was at that moment, to Jan's astonishment, that Adam began to cry.

"I've wasted thirty fucking grand on school. Thirty fucking grand." His mouth was twisted into a childlike pout. There was a sob in his voice. He was breaking down.

"What do you mean, *wasted*, Adam? Do you know what a degree from Harvard is worth?"

"A degree? Jan, I haven't been to a single class since the last week of September."

Jan felt her stomach lurch. She suddenly felt high again, too high to cope with Adam.

"I'm such a loser," Adam said. His head was in his hands. His skin now looked like the color of something edible, something fried. "I'm a loser. You should just forget about me." He looked at her with eyes that held no sorrow, only blankness. His mouth was twisted in his effort to hold back tears. His eyes alone held any color, and they were too bright a blue. Jan couldn't see beyond their brightness, to any message there. What did he want from her?

Yes, she thought to herself, I should. I should be done with you, Adam. I should walk away from here, from this mess, and feel no pity in my heart, just the strength in my limbs. She felt within her body a deep and rising disgust. That disgust was transforming itself into some newfound strength, and that strength was draining any sense of pity from her. She knew now what that silence had held. It was Adam's weakness flooding her, but she had fought it back. It had been horrible, but she had withstood it. Adam was weak. He was sick. He needed something she was never going to be able to give him.

She gazed back across the diner where Roberto sat. He was wearing a plain white T-shirt, a thick red and black flannel, and tan cords. It was odd that someone so ordinary-seeming had a friend like Stainless, someone everyone knew. He was sitting with a pale girl in a yellow sweater who sat slumped in her seat, either drunk or, like Adam, just depressed. As though he felt her eyes on him, Roberto looked over and did not look away—his eyes, Jan thought, held hers, just like that night when he came to her room with Eliza.

10

I t was only nine when Erika woke up and rolled out of bed. The sun shone through the raspberry-colored shade. The room still had Jan's choice of colors—a deep aqua wall, the raspberry shade, the rug composed of multicolored remnants Mom had found at some store in Brooklyn. The only change Erika had made to the room was to move her collection of Japanese manga onto the bookshelf and to hang a poster by her favorite manga artist. The poster depicted two girls with oversized eyes riding a moped through an intersection that was supposed to be in New York—Broadway and Third Avenue, but of course no such intersection existed. It was part of what Erika liked about Japanese manga; it didn't try very hard to be real.

Erika had discovered after attending a few parties with Binky and Morris that all parties were like costume parties, and usually nothing that happened at a party qualified as anything that had to be considered in the course of normal life. If Binky and

Christopher Primrose disappeared for an hour, it didn't mean Christopher would sit with Binky at lunch. If Morris didn't speak to her all evening, it didn't mean he wasn't going to play chess with her Monday. Parties were like the recess yard when they were little. People seemed to be moving all around her, while she stayed put, and spoke to whoever spoke to her. But she tried not to think too much about what she saw or heard. About the confusion of bodies.

The problem was that now something had happened at a party that she was required to consider in daylight. Something real had happened last night. Something horrible had happened to Melanie.

And Melanie had threatened to kill her.

This threat on her life was not something Erika could contemplate with Melanie sleeping off her hangover in the next room. Staring at the wall that separated the two bedrooms, Erika felt, rather than saw, a kind of pulsing in what should have been an imperturbable surface. It was a creepy feeling, like in a story by Edgar Allan Poe. Melanie's drunkenness, the incident with Gerald or whoever it might have been, and Melanie's low-voiced threat to Erika all seemed to accumulate in the physical space of the apartment. Erika knew when she felt her emotions bleed out in this way, into innocent and geometric spaces, that it sometimes helped to temporarily leave wherever she was.

Erika got up, dressed, and put on a heavy sweater. She knew she had to leave the apartment and clear her head, but first she texted Jan. Jan might know what to do. When they were young, and Melanie pulled Erika's hair or stole Erika's clothes, Jan had been a good mediator. Melanie listened to Jan. She kept the text simple, just said "call me," but she felt better even knowing that out there, somewhere, Jan was available to her, if not physically, at least in words. Words were not as soothing as colors could be, but Jan's words were better than most. She could picture the way Jan would hold the phone in her small, warm hands, and type back with her thin, white fingers. Jan had the prettiest hands, Erika thought. They were delicate, and reminded Erika of a pair of small, white birds.

Erika finished getting dressed and waved a brief hello to Julia, who sat at the dining room table typing away on some article or another. Erika didn't wish to disturb her mother, who, if she knew something was wrong, might want to talk, to detain Erika, when Erika knew what she needed was space and light, the rhythm of her own breath. Erika said she was going to go down to the Pain Quotidien to get a mocha, and she asked if Julia wanted anything. Julia declined a coffee, smiled distractedly, and asked Erika to take poor Max, the family's aging Yorkie, with her, which she did. Erika was thankful for Julia's businesslike manner, thankful she didn't ask too many questions about how and when they'd gotten home. Mom on deadline was the opposite of Mom at other times. The majority of the time, Mom was up for a chat, a cup of coffee, a long walk. Mom on deadline was mechanical, monosyllabic, and even a bit impatient when interrupted. Erika thought of her mother at such times as having a kind of on/off switch. On this particular day, she was happy her mom was switched off.

Maxwell was a good, silent companion on a day like this, and she could tie him up outside the café and still see him from the counter when she ordered. His presence, the rapid tapping of his dog toes against the pavement outside, somehow gave Erika a sense of calm.

The dog had no idea Melanie wanted to kill her.

Even with the brisk wind, Erika headed out toward the path by the river, wind hitting her in the face and blowing Max's fur straight back, ears and beard flattened, revealing his tiny mouth stretched into an oddly fixed canine grin.

The pedestrian walkway was uncrowded for a Sunday, probably because it was the day after Halloween and most people, like her sister, were still asleep. Erika thought about the party. For the most part, it had been fun. Christopher Primrose had held Binky's hand right out in front of everyone, which made Erika happy. She hadn't liked keeping Binky's secrets when the two of them disappeared into side rooms at Morris's. Morris had been funny. He drank a few beers, and when he did he reminded Erika of someone older, like his dad, who was fun to kid around with. She liked it when Morris's breath smelled like beer; it was a bitter, wheaty smell that reminded Erika of a sunshiny yellow, a color at once thin and bright, an aura, something to move through, and not merely see.

But the fun had come abruptly to an end when Erika and Jess had found Melanie in that terrible room with the bearskin rug. Before she'd even caught sight of Melanie's bare leg, she had seen that repulsive mouth—the frozen, wide-open mouth of death. She'd felt almost frightened to enter the room, afraid of what she might find. Then there was Melanie, so drunk she'd passed out, and her underwear pulled way down to her ankles. It was a pink, lacy thong, far fancier than any underwear she, herself, had ever owned. She had wondered even in that awful moment whether Melanie had bought it herself, or if Mom had gotten it for her.

Obviously, there'd been some sort of sex going on that maybe Melanie hadn't been completely awake for. This was upsetting to Erika, in the way that a complicated calculation, whose solution eluded her, might disturb her. She replayed the memory again and again, and yet each time felt she was missing some central component of the event. Was Gerald the boy? This was not really in question. He'd been just down the hall, and no one else was around. And Melanie was vehement about not taking him home. How the whole thing came to pass was also not really in question. Melanie had been very drunk, and these sorts of things happened. There were rumors she had heard about other girls.

Erika walked along by the gray, white-capped Hudson, with Max now panting at her side. The sun had risen higher in the sky and the air had grown warmer. It was undeniable that something had happened to Melanie that was unsafe, and Erika, as her older sister, should tell someone, should report the fact. But there had been that moment. Melanie had eyed Erika, clearly struggling against her own drunkenness, struggling to regain a single moment of clarity in which to deliver that horrifying threat to Erika's very existence; it was a moment that had frightened Erika more than any other moment of her life. Now she knew what people meant when they said "living in fear," for a fear of Melanie, and her power to retaliate against her in unrealized ways, had overtaken a number of her senses, dulling her mind with worry.

Since they were very young, Melanie had physically bullied Erika. She'd pushed and stomped. She'd smacked and pulled hair. She'd once deliberately, Erika thought, poked her in the eye with the sharp little foot of her Polly Pocket. Melanie had been only five at the time, but Erika remembered it. Even back then, Erika could recall knowing that she, herself, was incapable of those acts of violence her sister engaged in. Melanie hit at preschool too. When they were at the Park Preschool together, only one year apart, Erika recalled Melanie being the girl whom the other girls both loved and feared.

Erika never thought of hurting anyone. Her long, fine limbs, her own fresh radiant skin, gave her great joy, not because others found her beautiful, but because she found herself to be a resplendent being. She marveled at the workings of her fingers. Her knee joint contained the subtlest bones she'd ever seen, tightly wrapped in smooth, never ashy skin. Erika had a talent for solving difficult math equations, and she had a beautiful body, as sleek as a panther's. She couldn't hurt another being with this gift she'd been given by the universe.

Melanie's secret should be told for Melanie's own good, but

it would also feel good, for once, to not let Melanie intimidate her. It was a point Dad had often made, that she too often let Melanie push her around. Melanie was even bossy with Dad, making their father stop on his way home to buy her a particular brand of pen, taking the last bagel when she knew their father would want it. It's what Dad would want Erika to do if he were home. Dad was always reminding Erika that she had to stand up for herself, had to use her words.

But words had often led Erika astray. She owed nothing to the world of words.

When Jan called, Erika was on the side street near the Latin café, and she quickly grabbed a table.

"What is it?" Jan asked. Her voice sounded cloudy, and Erika hesitated, but only for a minute, before launching into the whole story about the punch and the boy with the eye patch, about Melanie's panties and Gerald all crooked and bent, puking in the glamorous little bathroom.

"Jesus," Jan said. There was an uncomfortable silence, a blankness Erika could almost see. "What should I do?" Erika asked, her voice rising in panic.

"I'm not sure yet," Jan said. "But if this only happened last night, I would stay out of Melanie's way at least for today. Let her rest. Then maybe I'll call her. Maybe I can get her to talk." Erika found herself nodding her head in agreement, instead of actually saying anything back to Jan. Of course Jan was right. Melanie needed sleep. She was tired, hungover, not in any way dangerous.

"But you'll call her right away?" Erika asked. "You'll call her tomorrow?"

"Well, yeah, I guess," said Jan. "The only thing is, Erika, she might not tell me anything. I can't just get in her business. It has to come from her first. You don't really know what happened, right?"

"But I do," said Erika, almost whining. "It was obvious. From what we saw. Binky and Jess think so too." It was difficult to hear every word Jan said. It was cold and windy. But there was something else about Jan's voice. She sounded muffled, or distracted.

"Okay," said Jan. "I still think it's tricky if she doesn't want to talk about it, Erika. Just let me process it, okay? I'll call her sometime soon. Right now, I've got my own crap to deal with."

There it was. Jan had something else going on. That was the way it was now with her family. Dad and Jan were away, leading their away lives. It wasn't true, what people said, about computers and cell phones keeping people connected no matter where they were on the planet. Where you were mattered. Especially with people. The people right in front of you were always the important ones.

Erika put her phone back in her pocket and looked down at little Max, who lay close to sleep on the cold sidewalk. She wondered what Max thought when people went in and out of his life. A dog's life, she thought, must be filled with panic.

When Erika got back to the apartment, Mom was on the phone in the kitchen talking to her editor. In fashion, they were already on to spring, and Mom had a great idea about what would be trendy in the warm months to come. Erika could hear her talking with bubbly excitement about pants—pants in every color, but especially pants that were yellow, gold, and sunflower, wide and flowing.

Erika let Maxwell off his leash and made her way back to her room, past Melanie's open door. Melanie sat at her desk. She had showered, and had her wet hair coiled on top of her head. She was wearing sweatpants and a long-sleeved T-shirt. She appeared to be doing her homework. Erika knew she should say something. She should at least ask how Melanie felt. But she was too much of a coward. Jan had let Erika down, basically saying whatever happened was Melanie's own business. But a crime wasn't one person's business. If that were true, there would be no law at all, no justice. No one would ever be safe.

11

"I thought we could just study? I have some research to do over at the Rock, but then we could get something to eat?" Jan was surprised by the sound of her own voice. She was pleading with Adam, when the night before she'd wanted to be far away from him, to never see him again, as if his depression or whatever it was that was causing his crack-up, were contagious.

Adam stopped stuffing his clothes into his backpack and looked up at Jan, a light wave of astonishment crossing his face. "Don't you remember last night, Jan? I confessed? Right? How I'm a total fuckup? From that moment on you treated me like a leper. I mean, it was like you didn't want me to breathe on you."

"Adam, we were on 'shrooms. I got upset. I can't explain it. It was like whatever dark mood you got into that made you feel like screwing up at Harvard. It was like I was there too, and I was just trying to get out. It wasn't real. It's not how I feel."

"Or, possibly, it's how you actually feel. And how you feel

right now, in the cold light of day, is like you're losing something. But it's just an idea. It's this idea you have of having a boyfriend and everything being all neat and tidy the way it's always supposed to be for Jan Russell."

Jan hugged her knees and contemplated Adam. It was hard to love him in that instant. His face had a sort of blurred appearance, like the mushrooms and exhaustion had removed the outline of his features, as though he were a drawing, partially erased, and she wondered if her own face had this quality.

"And I can't really understand this whole hurt act right now. I can't buy it. I feel like you hate me. You think I don't see it? But now you're the one crying. I don't get it."

"I never said anything like that to you. I never was critical of you."

"No." Adam sniffed. "No, you don't do that. You don't *say* anything."

"Adam, I thought you were acting weird. I mean about money and everything. But now I understand. You were upset, because of the money—"

"You mean the money I wasted by fucking up at school? You mean *that* money. How about the fact that this whole thing is fucked up? You and me, and your stupid-ass roommate, Eliza. Don't you see what a waste the entire system is? Nobody here knows what they're doing. Semiotics and women's studies. None of that changes anything, just gives a few pretentious assholes jobs. Then they lord this prestige over a bunch of stupid kids who've done nothing but listen politely and play by the rules their whole lives. Oh, maybe they dare to wear fishnets or all black or not wash their moldy-ass hair so their mommies get upset and cry. That's it. Brown is bullshit. I'm not saying I'm any better, or it's better in Cambridge. Seriously, I'm the worst, since I couldn't even play the game. It's a nice game, if you can play it."

Jan looked at her toes. She'd had a pedicure in September, but now the orange polish only partially covered each nail. She couldn't deny the absurdity of her life. A lot of what they did was ridiculous. Even in class, there was stuff that was hard to understand to begin with and even harder to fit into whatever it was her real life was supposed to be about. Did it really matter that people bought stainless steel appliances? What did it matter how many neglected novels by early twentieth-century female writers she read?

"Maybe we should be joining Teach for America. Or Habitat for Humanity, or one of those other groups. Maybe you're right to drop out. Maybe the rest of us are being robotic." Jan got up and started to pace the room. Ever since she'd gotten to Brown she'd felt mediocre, middle of the road—any of those descriptions for girls like her—girls who were pretty on a good day, but never beautiful, girls who were certainly smart, but never brilliant; thoughtful, but not radical. What was she meant for? What she was didn't seem to matter when she was surrounded by people like Eliza. Eliza was neither beautiful nor brilliant, but she thought she was doing something. She was committed.

"I'm sorry," Jan said finally. "I've been dealing with all the same stuff you're talking about. But I've pushed it down, and kept working and going out, and pushing all these questions away. I only look like I'm doing okay, Adam. But I'm right there with you."

Adam put down his bag and shook his head. He walked over to Jan and put his arms around her. His touch felt light, noncommittal. "No," he said. "You aren't having the same thoughts I'm having. But that's okay. You should keep doing what you're doing. You're meant for college. Don't worry. You'll do whatever you want to do." He put his bag on his shoulder. His eyes filled with tears and for a moment she thought he might cry. "I'm actually really surprised you don't see it yourself, Jan. I think, if things were right between us, you would."

"See what? See that you're freaking out at school? You don't know what you're doing there? See what, asshole?" She was shocked by the sound of her own voice. She could not recall ever calling anyone an asshole to their face before, and she dropped her head in instant regret.

"No," he said, shaking his head. His voice was flat. His eyes dull, expressionless. "You'd see that I don't give a fuck."

"About what? About me? About us?" Jan heard the alarm in her own voice and it made her heart beat faster.

"You don't see it, Jan, because to you all this feels like something. To me, I don't feel it. I can't understand why you can't tell how empty it is."

"You mean at home, when we planned this—you being nearby and everything? You didn't feel anything then? You were only going along with it?" Jan's whole body stiffened. It wasn't fair, what he was doing now. It couldn't be true. Even if he felt that way now, how could he take back everything they had been? How could he take back holding hands in the hallway, or sitting close on a park bench, or losing their virginity together?

"I don't know, Jan, what does it matter? I remember being happy. I mean, we were having sex. We were close. But that was high school. Doesn't it seem so long ago to you? And like we were all playing at something? None of that stuff matters now." He smiled faintly, as if his anger had run down like an out-of-gas engine. He reached over and took Jan's face in his hands. "I'm sorry. It's that everything feels like that to me now. You. School. I need to go back to New York for a while. I'm going to try to do something, get a job or something, and see what happens."

"Are you sure? Maybe you should go back to Cambridge. Find someone you can talk to?"

"No. I can't." Adam shook his head, and for a moment Jan thought he might change his mind, might take her in his arms and lie down with her on the bed, let her hold him, and tell him how everything was going to work out, how he was just stressed out. "No," Adam said. "I already cleaned my shit out and UPS'd everything home. I already got my train ticket. One way."

Once the door shut behind him, Jan sat up straight on her bed and stared at the space that Adam had occupied. He had known. He had known all weekend what he was going to do, and yet he'd gone through the motions with her. He'd already dropped out. He was on his way to New York. He had stopped in Providence on his way. Jan had difficulty catching her breath.

It had really been quite a show he'd put on for her—quite a performance. He had made it seem like it was all happening in the present and that it involved her, and what happened at the party, but in fact it had all already occurred. He'd already dropped out. He had made his decision, who knew how many weeks before, thinking about things that could not have had anything to do with her. Then he let her take him around town, buy the wine, drink in the loft party, and even take mushrooms together. Jan had not made Adam depressed on their 'shroom trip. He'd been depressed when he came to Providence. He had come to Providence to break up with her.

Jan sat on her bed, leaning against a pillow. Her body felt strangely light. The room, itself, seemed brighter without Adam in it. It was hard to believe they had really broken up. Jan felt tired. Her mouth was dry. Of course, there had been the 'shrooms, and now she had some sort of 'shroom hangover. She shut her eyes. Her phone buzzed from across the room but she could not rouse herself to see who it was.

12

The Monday after James Jamison's party was rainy and cold. Melanie was thankful for the miserable weather. It made her almost forget the true reason for her reluctance to get out of bed. Melanie was not one to fear the opinions of others, or to fret much over her social position. Rose Dyer was a small school and Melanie had been attending it with more or less the same group of kids since she was six years old. It was no secret that it was she, Melanie, who was often intimidating to the other girls, and not because she was one of those mean girls, like Lani Elliot, either, the kind who gets pulled into the principal's office because of the nasty things she's written in a bathroom stall. Melanie never really *did* anything to anyone. But Melanie never held back her opinion, either. If she was assigned to work in a group with someone useless, like Michelle Barnell, Melanie might roll her eyes. She might call her Barfnell, on occasion. But she didn't put much effort into these behaviors. It wasn't like she went home and went on the internet looking for pictures of hogs or hippos and posted them on Barfnell's wall. That sort of thing was for losers who didn't have better things to do with their time.

Normally, since Erika had moved into Jan's old room, Melanie relished her time alone in her own room. She had decorated her new daybed with little sequined pillows from Urban Outfitters. She'd gotten Mom to paint a cool accent wall—a sort of lavender color, on one side. And she had a view of the river. She loved lying in bed and looking out at the river and the lights of Jersey City as she fell asleep. She could see into hundreds of apartments in Battery Park City from her bed, and it was amusing to see how people lived. So many people did amazing things without even thinking to pull down the shades. There was Mostly Naked Yoga Girl, who did her sun salutations in just her panties. There was the dude almost directly across from her who sat in his living room in his boxers watching TV with his hairy belly hanging out for all to see. They didn't care. They were comfortable with themselves. These people didn't care what anyone thought of them.

The problem was that in this particular instance Melanie did care what people thought. She felt that if other people would stay out of it, she could keep her cool, and maybe forget everything that had happened Halloween night. But how could she forget if her own sister wouldn't stop staring at her? How could she forget when the rumors that were bound to spread were agonizingly true?

Someone who knew her had definitely seen her at the party, and knew what had happened, or at least knew that she'd been very, very drunk. Whoever it was had posted a video on Instagram and tagged her in it. The real clip was of a reality TV star staggering around in high heels, with her skirt hiked up so her panties showed. Obviously, no one would think that was actually her. Still, it wasn't a good sign, and when Melanie first saw the tag she'd felt a sudden surge of nausea and powered down her phone so she wouldn't have to look at it. She briefly considered dropping the phone out her bedroom window and pretending it had been an accident, but then she'd reconsidered. She was pretty sure no one had seen her in the room with the bear rug, except her sister and her friends. She had to go to school; she couldn't succumb to panic.

Of course, Melanie's biggest immediate problem was Gerald. As she chose her outfit she considered how she might act toward him. Should she shun him, or act like nothing happened? She pulled on a pair of baggy jeans and a tight-fitting off-white sweater. The sweater looked cool with the multistrand gold and silver necklace Mom had gotten her from some new accessories designer who was looking for her to plug her new line. Then she pulled on her tan motorcycle boots. They were from last year, but Melanie loved them. It was the first time all fall she'd taken them out. It was a good day for biker boots—rainy, cold—and she needed what they provided: an edge, a feeling of solidity.

"I made you two eggs this morning, hon. You ate almost nothing all day yesterday, so I thought you'd be hungry." Mom placed the plate in front of her—whole-grain toast and scrambled eggs. Erika was already eating a bowl of oatmeal. She had her hair up in a disgusting, messy ponytail and she was munching away, chewing with her mouth open. Erika was the most bizarre person on earth. That she was her sister, and that she was now privy to her awful secret, sent a shudder down Melanie's spine.

"Do you have to eat like that?"

"Like what?"

"Like a cow? Keep your mouth shut," Melanie said, then, pausing for emphasis, "I mean when you chew." Melanie hadn't even meant to threaten Erika with this double-meaning insult, it had just popped out. She had a certain genius, she thought, with this sort of thing, an odd intuitive power that told her exactly what words to use to get what she wanted from people.

She couldn't help that she had this power. She only hoped it would work as well as usual with Erika. Erika was stubborn and self-righteous, and that could work against even Melanie's bullying.

"Mel, we need to get something straight here. It was a big exhausting weekend for everyone. And we need to calm ourselves, okay? I am not going to make a big deal out of the fact that you were obviously feeling wretched yesterday, and I assume that was because there was drinking going on at the party. I'm not an idiot. But the reason I wanted you guys out together on Halloween is that it's safer that way. For sisters to give each other support. So let's just remember that? Whatever your differences, you're sisters." Mom looked tired. Her face looked thinner than usual, and she was wearing her stupid reading glasses perched at the end of her nose, which made her look owlish and old. Melanie felt a sudden disgust for her mother, for her glasses, her frown lines, her fading prettiness. But at almost the same moment, she felt a pang of remorse, of pity. Mom was getting old, and with Dad gone, she was as alone as anyone. As Melanie herself. This aloneness made her mother seem more her equal, even as it seemed to age her.

"Sorry," Melanie muttered contritely. "But maybe you can tell Erika to chew like a human being?"

Melanie made it her business to leave the house fifteen minutes earlier than Erika would. The last thing she wanted to do was take the subway with Erika. God knew Erika would try to initiate some conversation about what happened. That was to be avoided at all costs.

A few kids were hanging out in front of school, but not many. The rain had slowed to a drizzle, but most people had migrated to the cafeteria or to their homerooms. Students were encouraged at Dyer to hang out in the classrooms during their downtimes, and to chat with teachers. The whole atmosphere was chill, with kids eating lunch in classrooms, and asking for help whenever they wanted. In a way it didn't matter, though. Teachers were teachers, even if kids greeted them by saying "Wassup?"

Melanie trudged up the steps and pulled open the heavy glass door of the school's front entrance. There was no one in the lobby but the receptionist and a couple of teachers she didn't know. It had been a good call to get there early, so she didn't walk into the building with a whole crush of people. Once she saw Jess and went to her first couple of classes, the queasiness in her stomach would go away. She shouldn't have eaten those eggs, though. She'd wolfed them down to get on Mom's good side, since she knew she was being a bitch. She didn't want to add to Mom's worrying, or to let Erika get the upper hand at home.

When Melanie walked into room 307, only Gerald and Ray were already there. Ray was off in the corner, by the scrawny row of plants that nobody ever watered. Ray was a nobody—practically invisible, with sand-colored hair that was eerily the precise color of his eyes. But who had yellow eyes? It was one of those strange Ray qualities. In order to appear so perfectly indistinct, nature had evolved for him a unique shade of eye color. Ray, naturally, didn't look up when Melanie entered the room. He was too absorbed in whatever loser game he was playing on his iPhone. Gerald, on the other hand, was sitting there, as if he'd been waiting for her. He looked pretty bad, as though his hangover had lasted through to a second day. His hair was lank, and falling into his eyes. His forehead was covered with tiny red zits and he was wearing a faded gray Rose Dyer High soccer team T-shirt, stretched out at the neck and arms. Did he always look this shitty? Melanie wondered. As soon as he saw her, Gerald's face brightened into a taut, exaggerated friendliness. With a rehearsed-seeming formality, he stood up and walked over to Melanie's table.

"Can we talk?" he asked softly, his eyes cast downward. "Just for a sec?" Melanie was so taken aback she hardly knew what to do. She'd expected Gerald to behave oddly, but not like this. She hadn't expected that softness in his features, his obvious distress. He was wearing their shared disaster on his sleeve. His nervousness was so clear even a stranger, even a clueless teacher, would be able to tell there was something happening between them. Melanie felt herself flush. "No," she said. "I've got to finish my math." She took out her math book and began reworking a problem she had completed, hangover and all, on Sunday. To her surprise, Gerald didn't take the hint.

He stood there, drumming his fingers on her notebook. He pushed his hair out of his eyes. Melanie had never really looked at Gerald's face before, or maybe he'd never looked quite this way. His hair had gotten long—it came down over his ears and drifted in front of his eyes. His eyes were narrow, a light blue, not unattractive exactly, but there was something a bit rodent-like about his whole appearance.

Like a rodent, he was where he didn't belong.

They'd been friends a long time, and she had never really given him much thought. If she had to describe him, she'd have said he was reliable. Maybe a bit of a doormat. The sort of guy who had simply, conveniently, comfortingly, always been there. But this Gerald who stood drumming his fingers on her math notebook was not the same Gerald who'd come to her ninth birthday party and had given her all his extra tokens at Dave & Buster's. This wasn't the Gerald who'd let her ride his skateboard over to Jess's house while he jogged along beside her. This Gerald didn't seem to hear her.

"How about after school? I've got a newspaper meeting at

three, but maybe after that we could hang out, maybe walk over to the river?" Gerald looked down as he spoke. There was a certain weakness in his voice.

"Nope. I've got this project for English lit and I'm going to fail if I don't work for about ten hours straight on it. I'm not even done with the stupid book yet. *Jane Eyre*. Why is this book famous?" Gerald shook his head slowly, confirming he knew less than she did about *Jane Eyre*.

Everything Melanie said was true. She really was skipping play practice to go home and work. Not that her part really mattered. Lady Macduff. She had one scene and then she died. But that's what you got when you were a sophomore.

But the whole truth was that she couldn't wait to go home, to go home and get away from Gerald, to avoid Jess and her concerned glances. If everyone else would only forget the whole thing, she could forget and then it would be as if nothing ever happened.

But what was really annoying was Gerald in his stinking, stupid T-shirt, being super-obvious, being an idiot again, not leaving her side, giving her a headache. Why couldn't he just go?

"All right," he finally said. "I'll call you later." Oh God, Melanie thought. To say what? The only good news to come her way was when her mother said they were all going to Providence the following Saturday and Sunday for family weekend at Brown. Melanie needed to get out of town. She didn't care where, or even that she'd have to spend the weekend with Erika, who was practically her absolute worst enemy.

13

Mom had been a nightmare, as she always was about traveling, yelling at Melanie and Erika to get packed as soon as they walked in the door from school. Whenever they went anywhere, Mom transformed into a madwoman. Then, at Penn Station, they joined a horde of people at the Amtrak gate who looked like they'd been cast for one of those zombie apocalypse movies—one guy carrying a filthy leather backpack and an equally filthy leather-bound notebook nearly knocked Melanie unconscious on the escalator just by breathing on her. His breath stank of pure alcohol, fumes that made her recall all too clearly her own post-Halloween hangover, the feeling that her entire body was suffused with whatever your body produced when trying to rid itself of the poison, alcohol. She scrunched up her nose and searched over her shoulder for her mother and Erika. She did not want to end up alone in a seat for four hours next to a drunk creeper.

The actual trip wasn't too bad. Mom had paid to get them seats with a table, so they could get their homework done during the trip. At first, when Mom said they would all be going to visit Jan at Brown, Melanie had thought Dad would be there, too, but "all of us" now only meant everyone who was left. Melanie was disappointed Dad wouldn't be there. It made her think of all the times Dad might not be there with them when it actually mattered, like graduation or holidays. Mom had looked at her with surprise when she had asked about it, like Dad was in Hong Kong, and that was that. He'd emailed Melanie, of course, and asked about school, but he, too, was vague about when he might be coming back.

They arrived at the hotel at eleven. They had a big suite at the Biltmore, which was one of the only actual city-type buildings in downtown Providence. There was one room for Mom, and one for Melanie and Erika to share, but Melanie put her foot down.

"It's late, Mel. No one is asking you to move back in permanently with your sister, only to share a king-sized bed with her for one night." Mom stood in her worn black yoga pants and bare feet, hands on hips. Erika was already changed and in bed reading. Erika said nothing about having to share a bed with Melanie, although Melanie was sure Erika hated the idea as much as she did.

"Can't you call them and say there was a mistake?" Melanie asked. "It's a hotel. You're supposed to get what you want at a hotel, right? You pay for what you want."

"I said I'd take the two king beds. It's all they had. This is family weekend at Brown. Every place is fully booked. You'll live."

Melanie sighed, and then spied the couch in the sitting room. "I bet that thing folds out," she said. Mom finally got the picture that Melanie wasn't playing games, and she let Melanie make up the foldout couch with a blanket and spare pillows she found in the closet.

"That thing will murder your back," Mom said. "But if you insist, it's yours." Melanie lay in the darkness of the Biltmore suite. It was private, at least, on the dinky pullout bed. Mom and Erika closed their doors and she was alone with the lights from the city streets filtering through the curtains. She could close the heavier blackout shade, but she liked being in the semi-dark. Traveling alone with Mom and Erika was the last thing Melanie wanted to be doing. She and Erika were barely talking, and every time she caught Erika looking at her, Erika looked away with a frightened giant-mouse expression. Erika had those big eyes that seemed to always register panic. Why couldn't she have a normal sister, someone who had half a brain, and would know better than to keep staring at her in that annoying way? It made Melanie feel like a freak. Like what had happened on Halloween with Gerald had some visible, permanent consequence—as if she had shattered her spine. She could see now why bums on the street sometimes said stuff to you when you looked at them—*What are you staring at?* It was an invitation to a fight. But so was staring at someone like there was something wrong with that person. It made Melanie want to truly wring her sister's neck.

As hard as it was to be around Erika, it was good to get away, and not see Gerald or Jess or anyone else from school. Going places could erase the present, and turn it into the past. That's why people traveled, Melanie thought, to make their lives disappear, and then reappear, like a magic trick. When she went back home, she could get a fresh start.

Her mother was right that the pull-out couch was murder on her back, but her back had been aching her all day anyway. As she turned over on her stomach, she felt her breasts ache slightly against the hard bed frame, and realized that position was just as bad. She rolled back on her side and ran her hand down the length of her body. She was wearing a long T-shirt and a pair of boy shorts. She stroked her belly and her thighs, trying to press the achiness out of her body.

It had been a week now since the party. There was gossip, but she was good at ignoring gossip, and nothing else had appeared online after that one Instagram tag.

At first, her body had felt sore. There had been the hangover, of course, that seemed to go on for days. But there was the other soreness, too, inside and in her inner thighs. She had fooled around with boys before. There had been the usual kissing behind the school building with Bob Masur, and then she'd gone out with a boy from the neighborhood, Chase Lang, for a couple months last year. But going out with Chase had been no big deal. She'd gone to his house and watched a movie. One time, she'd been over there and they'd made out on the couch, and he'd taken her bra off, and felt her breasts, but when he'd reached for her jeans' button she'd told him to stop. She'd said she had her period, but that was a lie, and then they'd broken up over something stupid. The truth was, she was bored by Chase. She didn't like kissing him. He'd opened his mouth too wide, but she hadn't had the courage to tell him it was like kissing one of those white and orange fish that swim around the tanks in Chinese restaurants.

Thinking about the night with Gerald made Melanie blush with shame. She tried to push it from her mind, but for some reason the image of his drunken face kept rising in front of her. She remembered little from that night, but she recalled Gerald's looming, lumpy face, the look of concentration in his slate-blue eyes, the slackness of his mouth that came from drunkenness, and the slight flush in his cheeks that looked like pleasure. But maybe that wasn't a memory from that night at all, maybe it was a dream image, or an older memory of Gerald from some other time, some time when she'd made him happy by inviting him over, or by sitting close to him in the cafeteria. She knew Gerald had always liked her, and that their friendship was a bit of a sham. He'd do anything to be close to her.

She wondered whether people in other grades had heard about what happened, if Edward and his friends knew, and if so, what they thought. It wasn't fair that people talked about stuff that wasn't their business, or that you had to worry about other people saying you were a slut, a drunk ho, or whatever it was they'd say. People talked because they were bored and other people's fucked-up lives were like entertainment for them. Melanie Russell was a slut. It was a game to them to think of her like that.

It had been a crazy party. Lots of people were drunk besides her and Gerald, she was sure of that, though she didn't remember thinking about it at the time. She remembered so little she wasn't sure she could put together the full story, though the bits and pieces she did recall were vivid, even if they weren't completely reliable. There was the boy who laughed at her on the balcony. The red cup in her hand. The bear rug. And then there was Gerald. His touch was familiar at first, and made her want to laugh. It was silly to kiss Gerald. Silly and not much else. But then there was a strange moment when a rush of darkness whooshed over her, and she became very, very drunk, much drunker than before, and then there was Gerald, a part of that whooshing darkness, and her own body, and her own body whooshed, too—river-like, moving of its own will. It was like swimming and drowning at the same time. It was like being carried away, but it was also like being the water.

The aching in her back and breasts reminded Melanie that she was getting her period. Her period would come in a day or so, and then everything would truly be back to normal. She'd have no real worries.

She slid her hand down her belly once more, and thought, as she often did, about a boy. It was no one real, not exactly, though sometimes she realized there were parts of real people—a certain movie star's eyes—or, more awful and more secret, bits of people she knew, especially Edward—Edward's crooked smile, Edward's broad-shouldered body. It was wrong. Wrong. She knew that.

There must be something about her that was off—really perverted, and not like other girls, because even now, after what had happened with Gerald, Melanie couldn't control her own mind. In the darkness, her mind set itself free. She relished this feeling, her mind and her body moving as one in the dark; it always came back to this same feeling, and the feeling—she could not help it—was overwhelming and good. It was sometimes the only way she could get to sleep. She thought other people, especially other girls, must have easier brains, simpler lives, less messed-up dreams, more muted, less shameful desires. But maybe that wasn't true at all, and everyone was awful in this same way. It actually could explain a lot.

———

The next morning was bright and sunny, unseasonably warm for early November. After breakfast, if you could call a stale croissant and orange juice breakfast, they met Jan in the quad. They had been on their way to her dorm, but Jan had spotted them across the green, and ran over to them. She ran like a little kid coming home from camp. She threw herself at Mom and then Erika, pulling them close, but Melanie kept her hands at her sides and Jan gave her just a quick, little embrace.

"Oh, God, I'm so psyched to see you!" Jan said. Jan looked dramatically different, mostly in a good way. Melanie liked her haircut and eye makeup, and her clothes looked normal—jeans and a sweater, but everything looked a little tight. Jan and Melanie were the same body type, and Melanie took it almost personally that Jan had gained a little weight, as though this meant that she, too, was destined to be chubby in college.

"Let's go back to my room, and I'll show you around the dorm before we have to do the whole program. There's a few things we're supposed to go to—for information-type stuff—but then I want you to see the student art show, and then there's a poetry reading. I'm not reading. I was asked to, but I felt like it was too much. I mean, reading in front of other students is bad enough, but parents, no way." Jan was rambling and holding Mom's arm in a way that almost embarrassed Melanie. She looked around to see what the other freshman were like, but almost everyone Melanie saw looked really happy to see their families. She couldn't imagine herself at Jan's age being that excited to see Mom or Dad, but especially Mom. Mom was always around—too much so, and it was hard to imagine feeling excited to see her.

Jan's dorm room was cluttered with potted plants, posters, and stacks of books everywhere. Jan's roommate, Eliza, was there by herself, lying on her bed with headphones on, taking notes out of a huge book with a woman's face in profile on the cover. "Hey all," Eliza said, rolling off the bed and removing her headphones. "Don't mind me. I'm an orphan." Melanie was startled to see Eliza's hair was shorn on one side almost to the scalp. The girl had a sweet-looking round face, with round blue eyes, but then she had this extreme haircut, several ear piercings, and an eyebrow stud. Melanie wasn't opposed to the ear piercings, but the eyebrow piercing made Eliza look like the New York City kids who hung out on Fourteenth Street, not like someone who went to a really good college.

Mom put her hand out to shake Eliza's hand and Eliza wiped her hand on her black and tan miniskirt and then shook it. There was a bag of half-eaten corn chips on the bed. "I've been drowning my sorrows in trans fats," Eliza said.

"Eliza is from Montana, and her parents couldn't come out," Jan explained. Melanie could see Eliza made Jan nervous. She smiled to herself thinking of her perfect sister living with this tall girl in fishnet stockings with her half-shaved head. "This is my sister Erika, and my other sister, Melanie," Jan said.

Eliza raised her eyebrows. "Well, aren't we an attractive bunch!" Eliza said. "There must be something in that New York City water that makes everyone there a sex bomb. Or maybe it's just the fat thing. My people have huge asses. It's like you spend a few winters in Montana, and your body starts trying to cover as much ground as possible. I don't know why. It's like you become part of the landscape."

"Perhaps it's to stay warm," Mom offered lamely. But Melanie stayed quiet, unsure, around this steamroller of a girl.

"That's not how adaptation works," Erika said. "Regional trends are usually about diet." Erika was wandering around the dorm room, flipping through Jan's books. She was wearing a gray sweatshirt and a pair of jeans that were too loose around the waist, and had her hair in a ponytail. If you didn't know Erika, she looked cool, confident, like one of those beautiful girls who dressed down, as if they were unaware of their obvious advantage.

Eliza eyed Erika. "So where are you applying? MIT? Yale? Some genius clusterfuck?" Mom raised her eyebrows.

"Eliza!" Jan said sharply, shaking her head.

"Oh, Jan's Mom, I'm so sorry! I was raised by wolves. Seriously, people in my family are completely tacky. We have zero class." Eliza went over to Mom and gave her a little hug. She was statuesque, but not thin, with a belly that protruded slightly from beneath a too-short sweater. Her asymmetrical hair was dyed red and she wore heavy black eyeliner. Melanie tried to imagine Eliza with normal hair. She thought she would be pretty, prettier than Jan, and maybe even than Melanie herself. She had a tattoo on one hand that was shaped like a gecko or some other lizard. She caught Melanie eyeing the tattoo.

"Like it?" Eliza asked. "That's Fred. I had him for five years and then my cat ate him. Our cat is like this giant half-bobcat thing. He was really cute when he was little, all fluffy like a regular cat, but the vet said he must be the product of some feral housecat and a bobcat, and so now we live with this dangerous animal. Last year, he knocked the top off Fred's cage and ate every last bit of him. I took a picture to the tat artist and he did this for me. There was nothing my parents could say, because they know it's insane to live with this creature prowling around the house at night. My mom keeps him in the house so he won't get the chickens."

All three of the visiting Russells stared at Eliza. She hadn't stopped talking since they'd walked in, and it was hard to assess if anything she said was true. Jan sighed loudly. She seemed used to being in Eliza's shadow. Melanie wondered how she would deal with a roommate like that. She looked from Eliza to Jan. Then, for a second, Jan caught Melanie's eye, giving her what Melanie took to be a questioning glance. Melanie quickly looked away. But then Jan went back to being their tour guide.

"Well," Jan said, "I think we're going to do the Campus Walk and then go around to the reading at the Spanish House." She hesitated a moment. "You can come if you want," she said to Eliza.

"No, thanks," Eliza said. "But maybe I'll catch up with you later? There's this protest thing over on West Quad tonight at eight." She turned to Mom. "It's an annual thing we do—a Women and Allies March. It's every Family Weekend. It's in the slut walk tradition. We're trying to get rid of these cretin frat guys—gain awareness among all the families that these Neanderthals still walk the earth. You know, the 'no means yes, and yes means anal' types?' Just got to slam that shit."

"I'm not sure I've heard of that type," Mom said, half laughing. "Certainly, the first part, but not the latter. Anyway, date rape is the oldest problem on campus. I'm glad you girls are aware of that." Mom was being annoying, sucking up to Jan's weird roommate. Or was that comment meant for her? What was going on? Melanie wondered. It seemed like all eyes were on her, like both Jan and Erika were staring right through her. It was like she lived in a family of mind readers.

"Jan's Mom, it's the oldest problem period. Dudes act like the penis is a power tool with no off switch." Eliza shook her head. "Jan, you should bring the little Russell chicklets. They need their heads on straight now. High school is when girls get groomed to think boys are their salvation on earth. Those proms and dances and football games and cheerleaders with their ass cheeks hanging out. Ugh. It is one giant grooming enterprise to disempower women and make them worship dick. Get them thinking their asses belong to the biggest, fastest, genetically high-performing male organ, like some sort of stone-aged pri-mal orgy. That's high school, fucking prehistoric. Getting them ready for the frat-house gang bang." Eliza paced around the room, getting her coat and packing her bag while ranting about high school.

Melanie could feel her heart skip a beat. Who was this girl? Melanie wondered what Montana must be like to have bred an Eliza. She thought about Rose Dyer High School, about Gerald and the party. Dyer didn't even have a football team. James Jamison's school probably did, though. The uptown schools, Melanie thought, might be more like Montana. But still, what Eliza said gave Melanie a nervous feeling in the pit of her stom-ach. She felt tears welling up in her eyes, and her throat constrict. She knew Eliza couldn't possibly know what was going through her mind, but did Jan? She had to put a stop to it somehow. She felt like in some bizarre way everything Eliza said was meant for her, and that her whole silent family was interrogating her.

"I don't think that's true," Melanie suddenly heard herself say. Everyone looked at her, Erika staring her inescapable stare.

"Well, honey . . ." Eliza began.

"No. I mean some guys maybe. But not all guys. Anyway, sometimes it's the girls too. Not like what you said about frat parties, I'm not talking about really awful stuff like that, but I know girls who brag about their hookups, you know, keep lists," Melanie stammered. She wasn't sure what she was trying to say. She thought about Lani Elliot. She thought about Gerald. Gerald had always been afraid of her. Could he also have been, as Eliza suggested, just waiting for an opportunity? But didn't that make him more pathetic than anything? "I don't know about where you went to school," Melanie said finally, "but at my school it's not like that. Guys and girls are pretty much equal. I think girls are responsible, too, for things that happen. . . ." Melanie trailed off, still uncertain of what she meant.

The room went silent. She hadn't ever fully formed the thought before, that what had happened with Gerald was in part a result of her own actions, her drunkenness, but maybe something more. If it hadn't been Gerald, she wondered, would it have been someone else? She remembered the tall, good-looking boy, and the cruel way he had laughed at her. She had tried her best to push the entire episode out of her mind, but now here she was, blabbing to Eliza from Montana, and saying she didn't know what.

"You see, Jan? Jan's mom? I bet you think if a girl's wasted it's what she deserves if a bunch of guys do her and tape it?

And everyone in ten countries watches on YouTube? She totally deserves the slut-banging and bashing. That's what you're saying. That's the Western Taliban, right here in the United States of Assholes. We don't stone girls, we *film* them." Eliza paused either for effect, or to breathe.

"But I'm not going to rag on you anymore, honey, because you're still a baby girl and there's time for you. But you there, big sis, you need to come tonight. We're going to dress up in insane in-your-face stuff and walk the walk, like serious hoes. Because that's the point, little sister. You should be able to rock it all the way off." She paused again and pointed her finger directly at Melanie. "And no motherfucker frat boy can take his dick out unless you say he can. *First.* That's rules one through ten right there."

"Okay," Mom said. "On that note, I say we go get our tour, and some lunch. Enough consciousness raising for one morning." All three girls turned and looked at Julia Russell, who'd remained silent for most of Eliza's rant. But Melanie could see her mother at least in part approved of the conversation. If she hadn't, wouldn't she have stopped it? Melanie took a deep breath and turned back to Jan, who threw her a quick glance as she grabbed her backpack. Jan looked impressed, Melanie thought. Impressed that she'd stood up to weird Eliza. Maybe Jan did know about her, Melanie thought. But if she did, she wasn't saying anything. Good. Melanie stood a little straighter. Jan was the only sane member of her family. The only one who remotely understood her.

Outside, the sun was bright and the air was warmer. There

was a slight, earthy smell to the air now, where earlier it had simply been crisp. Melanie followed behind her mother and Jan, who had linked arms. Erika walked alone, too, but a few steps ahead, gazing at the brick buildings that lined the quad. It was a pretty campus. The buildings were old, some white stone and some brick, but none looked imposing. Melanie could imagine going to school in such a place, but she knew Brown would be out of her reach. But if Eliza were the typical Brown student, Melanie thought she might want to go someplace more mainstream.

Eliza had said she was wrong to think things might be her own fault, at least a little bit. She said it like that was ridiculous or worse, like it was a crime, and she, Melanie, had been brainwashed, was already some kind of robot girl. No, it didn't make her feel better to think she was a victim of the male species, especially not the way Eliza said it, which made her feel stupid.

It made her feel dizzy to think about it, and somehow, she felt even guiltier. Now Erika, and maybe Jan, too, thought girls who went to those kinds of parties, and had stuff happen to them, were stupid, worthless people who let guys ruin their lives. Eliza had said there was still time for her, but there wasn't. If Eliza and Jan were right about stuff, she was already one of those girls, and she wasn't sure how or if a person could change that. If she'd been so stupid already, maybe that was just who she would always be. She knew she wasn't a smart girl like Jan or Erika, and she had always wanted to go to parties like James Jamison's. It was just that the party had gotten a little too out of hand. . . . But now she didn't know.

Melanie felt warm out in the bright sunshine and she wished she hadn't worn such a heavy sweater. She felt an ache in her back again, and then a sudden rush. She felt a wave of nausea, and with that wave came an emotion. It was revulsion. She pictured Gerald's pale face. His grimness at school, his staring at her in English. She felt another wave. She knew this feeling. She'd had it often toward Erika, even toward Mom sometimes. It was hate and it was absolute.

She wished she had hit him when she had the chance, hit him hard, so his mouth swelled, his nose bled. She wished it was him who had been found on the stupid white rug, bloody, in pain. She wished that wicked, dark wave of desire had made her strong and not weak. No, she thought, no matter what Eliza said, it wasn't too late for her, and she wasn't a brainwashed girl. She was filled with hate. But hate was something Melanie knew how to deal with. She stood up a little straighter and tossed her hair. She stopped and shifted her purse higher up on her shoulder.

She wasn't going to let a stupid boy like Gerald, and those stupid people at school with their idiotic Instagram accounts, make her feel worthless. Maybe Eliza was right about some things, but maybe there was something wrong with what she said too. But right now, she didn't want to know what anyone thought about anything. She wanted everyone to shut up. She felt another wave of nausea, but it wasn't hard to ignore now. Her back ached again, too, but this time she knew why. She had gotten her period.

14

The tour of the Brown campus had been wonderful. Erika particularly liked the engineering and biology buildings, which were, as they should be, in the exact center of campus. The engineering building was tall, a tower, and the biology building wound itself around like a maze. She loved this too. Still, Brown was not her ideal school. There was a strangeness to the quad area that Erika did not like. There were kids who seemed to be sitting around with little to do, the way you sometimes saw kids in the city, kids who lacked purpose. Erika could deal with people who weren't like her, who didn't know what they were supposed to be doing in life. That was most people, anyway. No, what she didn't like about Brown was its slant. The whole campus occupied a side of a hill. If Erika went to a hillside campus, she would want the campus to go all the way over the top of the hill, and not to merely hang off the hill on only one side, the way Brown did. It would make her nervous, she felt, to be hanging there. It would be altogether better to go someplace that was simply flat.

After the day on campus, Erika, Jan, Mom, and Melanie had an early dinner, though Melanie said she didn't feel well, and just moved her pasta with meat sauce around her plate, unjustly committing at least one unfortunate cow to a second annihilation—first its animal life was taken, and then it failed to be eaten as dinner. In the interest of keeping the peace with Melanie, Erika restrained herself from saying something about eating what had been murdered for her wasted culinary pleasure.

But then the most exciting thing had happened. Melanie and Mom went back to the hotel, and Mom agreed to let Erika spend the night in Jan's room. Erika had a spare toothbrush in her purse, and everything else she needed she could borrow from Jan.

"I'll text Eliza," Jan said. "You can sleep in my bed, and I'll use my sleeping bag and camping pillow on Eliza's. I'm sure Eliza can find someplace else to sleep. She does it all the time." Jan rolled her eyes when she said this.

"Oh," Erika said. "I thought she didn't like girls who, you know, hooked up." She and Jan were on their way to the protest that Eliza had told them about earlier. But they weren't there really to protest, more to watch. As they approached West Quad, they heard the beat of drums, and other instruments, a flute, perhaps, and a tambourine. It was dark and a crowd was gathering, so it was difficult to see exactly what was happening. On one side, there seemed to be a group of boys sitting sprawled on the steps of what Erika assumed was a fraternity house. The boys weren't doing much of anything, just sitting, some with red cups in their hands. She smelled pot, too, and she wondered whether the campus police would soon arrive, or did these things go unacknowledged, the way they did on city streets?

"Oh, I don't know where Eliza stands on guys," Jan said. "But she likes girls, no doubt." Jan kept walking until they stood on the outer edge of the crowd across from the frat house. One boy held a sign that said *We love lesbos* on it. Some boys yelled for the girls to kiss. They all seemed to be watching the girls eagerly, without shame. They didn't seem aware that they were being protested against.

In the area in front of the frat house a group of girls marched in fishnets, thigh-highs, heels, bras, thongs, and leotards. One heavyset girl had cut out two holes from a black leotard, so that her nipples showed, but these she had covered with colorful stick-on tassels, which twirled as she walked. The boys jeered at her. One boy pretended to vomit. Another girl wore a shiny gold bikini. She was tall, with dreads and a flat stomach, small breasts, and long limbs, like Erika, herself. She wore only the gold bikini and a pair of high heels, though it was a cold night. Across her chest was written in bold black letters the single word: *Raped*. At first the boys were silent as she passed, and then one boy staggered onto the top step of the frat house and yelled "You loved it! Bitch!" over and over again, until one of the other boys threw a cup of beer at his head, and then lunged at the boy's knees, tackling him so that both boys rolled off the porch and into the bushes, where Erika could hear yelling, but could no longer see either one of them.

For a moment, the small parade stopped in front of the rest of the boys and the tall, pretty dreadlocked girl just stood there in front of them and the rest of the girls marched around her, some banging on drums, with one petite brunette in a thong, a football jersey, and go-go boots playing the flute. Erika saw Eliza, wearing the same skirt and fishnets she had on earlier in the day, but with a black fisherman's cap, a black leather jacket, and a red and black bustier replacing the cropped sweater. She was standing talking to one of the boys, whose hair was tousled—perhaps the boy who'd knocked the other boy from the porch—and he seemed to be listening earnestly to her with his arms across his chest. He had on a button-down shirt and had dark hair. He carried no sign, and held no plastic cup. He smiled in a friendly way at the nearly naked girls who marched in circles in front of him.

Soon, a simple chant rose up among the girls: "*End campus rape*," with the tall girl still standing in front of the gaping boys, and the other girls circling around her. Then, a blond girl, wearing short shorts and motorcycle boots, began going from one girl to the next, writing *raped* across each girl's forehead. Some of the boys kept up with their own chant, "*Kiss, kiss, kiss, show us your tits, tits, tits!*" But then the short-haired boy who had been speaking to Eliza went over to the crowd, and Erika could see him shaking his head, and then the boys went silent.

Gradually, more scantily clad girls appeared with markers,

made their way through the crowd of regularly dressed kids, and began writing the word *raped* across everyone's heads. The crowd included both boys and girls and almost everyone submitted, allowing the girls to write in bold, neat letters across their foreheads. Erika saw the little blond girl getting closer to her and Jan, and she reached out and grabbed Jan's arm, but the crowd had gotten dense, and some people were moving closer to the girls with the markers, and other people were trying to get away, and Erika lost her grip on Jan.

Erika wanted to get away, but not without Jan, who had been swallowed up by the crowd. Erika pushed forward and again reached out to grab Jan's jacketed arm. Jan had been wearing a suede jacket. Something dark brown. Finally, she saw her. She reached out and put her hand around Jan's forearm, pulling her close. Most of the time, Erika avoided physical contact, even with her sisters, but now she wanted to hug Jan, for Jan to hold her hand, for them to run away out of the crowd together. At first, Jan was stuck, but then she made her way through, and was moving closer to her.

Then, suddenly, Erika felt a full mouth on her own, soft and welcoming. She was being kissed, but was utterly unaware of anyone having approached her. It was a kiss unlike any other. There was a flavor to it, like lemon and cardamom. Then Erika broke free.

The girl in front of her had short brown hair and freckles across her nose. She was wearing a suede jacket, like Erika had imagined Jan wearing. The girl had the awful word scrawled across her forehead, and once she removed her mouth from Erika's she held the marker up to write it on Erika's face as well.

"No, don't!" she heard Jan say from somewhere in the dark. "That's my sister!" But Erika had put her hands up to her forehead just in time, and the girl had only gotten the backs of her hands. After that, Jan appeared miraculously next to her. Jan knew the girl with the freckles who had kissed her. "Sarah, don't, that's my sister. She has to go home tomorrow! This shit doesn't come off!" Jan was laughing.

"Oh, sorry," Sarah said. "I think I kissed your baby-dyke sister! Oh, I'm a corrupter of innocents!" Sarah covered her face in mock horror. Jan shook her head.

"Well, there's your first taste of college, Erika," Jan said as she patted her shoulder. "Don't worry, you'll survive, like the rest of us. Barely."

"No, it was fine," Erika said, flustered, and she covered her mouth in embarrassment. The older girls laughed, and Erika looked away. She usually didn't like kissing, or the idea of kissing. But this kiss that came out of the dark, and was followed by this freckled girl, was a little like those cheap toys that come with fast-food meals. It was something she hadn't expected, hadn't wanted, but it had made her heart leap a little, although she couldn't begin to say why.

15

Morris Foster's bedroom was filled with birds.

He had three parakeets and a cockatiel, all of which darted freely around the room. The male parakeet, a blue one, liked to perch on Morris's head, but the two females, one yellow and one white, preferred the sides of the cage and the wooden slats of the window blinds. Erika liked the birds, but feared the male. Once, when she was younger, the male had dive-bombed her head and had been caught in her hair. Foss had had to come in and "get the damn bird out of that white-girl hair." After the ordeal, Erika had taken a shower to wash the bird crap out of her hair. She remembered Foss had let her use his shower because the boys' bathroom was only fit for a couple of "stink boys." Foss's shower had smelled nice, like pine needles. He had given her two plush towels to dry off with. The towels had been black. Erika had never seen black towels before, but she figured maybe if you were a rich, single guy that's what you used. Morris's mother had never been around as long as

Erika could recall. There was a vague story of an illness when Morris was very young, but Erika wasn't sure if the woman had actually died or had become incapacitated, whether the illness had been physical or mental, and it was now much too late to ask. Morris's mother had been a talented and beautiful singer, that was all she knew.

The blue bird sat on top of Morris's head as Morris sat playing Gun Metal on his computer. Every so often Morris banged his hand on his desk and the bird momentarily took flight like a cartoon bird, landing again once Morris calmed down. Morris didn't worry about bird crap on his head since he kept his hair so short it was almost shaved.

"I don't know, Erika. Just don't know. Why don't you talk to her? Get the whole story." Morris bounced in his chair as he spoke.

"That's the point. She'd never tell what happened. If she even knows. You didn't see how drunk she was, Morris. You weren't in the room." Binky was curled up in the corner of Morris's room, working on a math problem. She looked concerned, though, and Erika was thankful for that. Binky chewed on the end of her pencil and brushed a piece of long blond hair out of her eyes. "What do you think, Erika, would Melanie ever talk to you?"

Erika stared hard at Binky. Binky was lucky, even with her hearing problem. She had full lips, deep brown eyes, that long hair—of course, Erika was a sometime model, a beautiful girl herself, but Binky had changed in the last year. Somehow Binky had figured out how to make Christopher Primrose like her. Maybe it was that simple trusting look she had. She didn't doubt people like Erika did. Erika never seemed to know what other people would do—even when she thought really hard about it beforehand. Who would have thought Melanie would have done what she did at the party? Who would have thought that freckled girl would kiss her at Brown, and that she, Erika, wouldn't be disgusted? Would have enjoyed it? And then there was Gerald. She'd known Gerald for years, and he was one of the few boys at school who never made Erika feel nervous. He was "just Gerald." That was the way Melanie had always referred to him. He never struck Erika as a dangerous sort of boy.

"I don't know. But I think someone should be told, like my mom, or Ms. Jensen in the guidance office. Then they can figure it out. I mean, assuming Gerald is the one who raped her." Morris suddenly stopped playing Gun Metal, and Binky put down her math book. They both stared at Erika. Erika thought back on the protest at Brown. She wished Morris and Binky had been there, too, had seen that word, spelled out in black across the tall girl's forehead. It was like a sign, although Erika tried not to believe in superstitious things. More like it was just reality, and it wasn't hiding any longer in the corner of her mind.

"Yo. That's no word to throw out like that, girl. You can't just go telling the guidance counselor or your mom someone did your sister! You don't even know the whole story. Maybe she wanted to fuck the dude? Ever think of that?"

"She was drunk, Morris, she couldn't have said yes."

"I'm just saying—once you use that word the kid is toast, and

I never thought he was a bad kid. And just because he was in the bathroom down that hall, that was not the scene of the crime, you know? Anyway, don't they hang out—maybe they hooked up and you don't need to sweat it? Melanie is a down girl." Morris stared at Erika shaking his head, making her feel stupid. She hated when Morris did that. He never did that when they were working on a science project, or doing math together—then she had his respect. But now Erika felt like a loser. Melanie was her sister, after all. She would know it if she were dating someone, or if she were "down," whatever that meant. It wasn't up to Morris what she decided.

"I think maybe Erika is right. Maybe we should tell Ms. Jensen that something happened, that we don't know what exactly, and then she can call Melanie into her office and talk about it. Melanie will be upset, but she maybe would thank you someday, Erika, for watching out for her." Binky was agreeing with Erika, but she looked all twisted-up and uncertain, whereas Morris sounded sure of himself, and seemed angry.

"I think it was just a bad scene at that party, and we should let the two of them work it out and mind our own business, assuming that's the dude in question," Morris said. "Seriously." He shook his head and turned his attention back to his game, seemingly setting the matter to rest, although he tapped his foot nervously, like he was still angry about the whole topic.

Erika stood up and began walking around Morris's room, causing the birds to all chirp and flutter. She had her hair pulled back and wrapped up on top of her head, which made her feel even taller than usual. She looked out Morris's window at the river. It had stopped raining and the sun played off the white-caps. She wished she really believed in signs, like if the sun went back behind a cloud, emailing Ms. Jensen was a bad idea, and if the sun brightened again, it was the right thing. She wished there were always right answers, and signs out the window. She wished she knew what it meant that a girl had kissed her and she'd thought about it nearly a hundred times since—thought about kissing that girl back, and about the freckles on her nose. Did that mean she, Erika, was a lesbian? If she was one, what should she do about it? She wished she knew the answers to these questions, so she could stop thinking about them once and for all.

She was so good at arriving at right answers, but people had been telling her all her life that with some things, there were no absolutes. That's what her fifth grade teacher, Elizabeth, had told her about reading, that what the author was saying was meant to be unclear sometimes, ambiguous. But it didn't really matter in books if things were unclear. No one hated the author forever for leaving everything up in the air, or for keeping something shameful a secret.

Melanie had told Erika she'd kill her if she breathed a word of what happened at the party, and a part of Erika still believed her—not that she would kill her, but she would harm her in some way—seek revenge. But her initial panic of that day had subsided. Mel had refused to share a bed with her in Providence. She'd been standoffish to everyone on the visit, except maybe Eliza.

How could she, Erika, know the truth and do nothing? How could Gerald, who'd been hanging around with Melanie since third grade, hurt her and not pay for it? Maybe Melanie needed someone to help her, even if it made her angry. It was clear Melanie was confused. She needed someone other than Eliza to talk to. Someone who didn't go writing on people's heads. Someone who knew all about these things, and could explain them the right way—an adult, a counselor, someone who'd read books and had gotten degrees in things like psychology that explained people to themselves, and who knew what to do when things went wrong and how to make them right again.

"I don't know, Morris," Erika said. You know that time you said I was ignorant because I'm white? I'm thinking maybe now you're not getting this because you're a guy. You keep defending him." Erika was surprised by the sound of her own voice. She was calm, but when she spoke there was no concealing her anger. Morris straightened up, pushed his chair back from his desk, and let out a deep sigh. He looked at Erika gravely and shook his head.

"Girl," he said, "you've known me a long, long time. Since grade school. Don't you have any idea when I'm talking shit?"

Erika shook her head. "No," she said. "I guess I don't. So, what are you saying? White people aren't really ignorant? Or guys aren't?"

"What I'm saying is you and me both, Erika. We don't know jack shit."

16

Jan was without a boyfriend for the first time in three years. She had no obligation to anyone but herself. The Adam she loved—the calm boy who'd strolled around New York City holding her hand, the boy who never pushed her into sex, but waited, intensely, watchfully, until she was ready—that calm, sweet boy had been transformed into a self-absorbed college guy who was too neurotic to really care how she felt anymore. She couldn't recreate the old Adam.

For the first time since middle school, Jan felt kind of boy crazy. One night at the Rock, she'd seen Roberto. At first, she hadn't recognized him. He was with another guy, a short boy with blond hair. He'd said hello in the drafty glass entranceway, and asked her what her name was. He reintroduced himself, muttered something about knowing he knew her from some-where, and then he'd walked away.

She knew almost nothing about Roberto, but every time he

looked at her, every time she saw him somewhere unexpected, it made her day. Andy mocked her for not going up to him and starting a conversation. She couldn't, though. She told herself it was too soon after Adam, but really she was too nervous.

———

Jan was so jumpy and pathetic these days whenever she went anywhere on campus, it was reassuring to be sitting in her dorm room reading and munching oven-baked vegan black-bean chips with Eliza, who, finally, had stopped wearing fishnets and put on an actual pair of pants—slouchy black pinstripe trousers with suspenders, but pants nonetheless. It was like after the high drama of the anti-frat slut walk, Eliza had mellowed out and put less energy into appearing radical. Jan was reading a novel for her Neglected Woman Novelists class, but Eliza kept interrupting.

"I can't believe it's fucking November," Eliza said. "I mean, I have been here almost two months and I have been laid—do you want to know how many times I have been laid?"

Jan shook her head. She wasn't sure what even counted with Eliza as "getting laid." She was pretty sure she had been with both guys and girls at various different times, but it was hard to tell with Eliza. She always seemed to be doing something illicit—drugs, sex, over-the-top protests—but you never knew. The girl had actually been sitting in the room as long as she had—at least four hours—so maybe some of those nights when she disappeared to some girl's or guy's dorm room, they'd really only been hitting the books.

"Well, it's freaking sad. Because the truth is zero. Zero fucking times laid since I have been here at Brown! I cannot believe myself."

Jan looked up. "Really?"

"Yep. I know you always figured I was some slutty Montana bitch, but I have not taken my panties off except to pee since I got here. These Brown guys are all either predators or monks. There are all these hot guys, but they never leave the research stacks in the Rock and are probably jerking off in there because they're scared to death of the sight of an actual vagina. This whole place is like divided in two—half are these monastic cells where people beat their hard-ons down with copies of the Oxford English Dictionary, and the other half are these dens of total iniquity where everyone is like a walking, talking boner. You can't converse with a penis. It's just impossible. It's definitely getting on my nerves."

Eliza paused, but Jan only shook her head, speechless as usual. She wondered where it was that Eliza actually hung out. It was like she occupied a parallel universe in which everyone was engaged in some sort of bizarre sex act.

"There was only this one time that was even slightly close, with this guy from Dialectics. Dark curly hair. Really pale skin. He wears tan cords practically every fucking day. It's like a pants fetish. But he's got amazing eyes. You know that green-blue color in the crayon box? With girly-long lashes. And just enough stubble so you know you're not sucking face with a chick. He is so insanely attractive, I am completely willing to overlook the pants for his undying devotion, or at least a night's devotion. An hour's devotion. Fifteen ecstatic minutes, maybe. His name is Roberto. Wait—I think you met him? He's kind of chubby? Well, I saw him at a party down near Wickenden and we were both wasted, and we ended up back at his room, totally in the moment. Heat of and shit. Getting almost beyond the point of no return.

"But then I could tell he was hesitating, you know, not sure if I was okay with it. At least that's what I was hoping, and not that he was totally repulsed by me or something. So I froze. Asking myself all kinds of questions. Getting all in my head. And, wanting-it-bad babe that I am, I could not think, in that critical moment, of the freaking word for yes. And then the moment was gone. Amazing, really, how small the moment can be. Now I can't bring myself to ask the hottie for coffee even though I see him three friggin' hours a week." Eliza was lying on her bed with her feet resting against the dorm-room wall, scuffing the paint with her dirty socks.

Jan's heart sank in her chest. A chip felt lodged in her throat. Why did it have to be Roberto? She shook her head, then forced a laugh. "That is a really sad story, Eliza." She hesitated for a moment, torn between thinking it was fortunate for her Eliza hadn't gone further with Roberto, and feeling selfish for thinking so. After all, she didn't really know the guy. Jan's crush was pure fantasy, while Eliza was confiding an actual experience. "You can't ask him out for coffee? What's with that?" she asked, recovering enough to appear sympathetic. Jan had been thinking almost obsessively about Roberto for the last week. But alas, Eliza was claiming him first.

"I dunno," Eliza said. "I am completely insecure with guys I actually like. So that could be a small factor, my total inability to speak to him."

"Well, then," Jan asked, redirecting the conversation, "what about the Brown girls?" She'd always thought Eliza preferred girls, and now that she thought they might be in some direct competition, she hoped she was right.

"I got over that lesbo shit in high school—not that I care who wants to go all dykey here, but, I mean, there's just no *challenge* there for me. You know, like the sight of a vagina does not excite me anymore. I guess it's the kind of thing that matters when it's your first? First joint, first fuck, first dildo—but, seriously? I cannot get it up for that shit."

She wasn't sure what she had done to prompt this confession from Eliza, but there it was. She laughed. It was entertaining to have Eliza for a roommate. It kept Jan from having to think too much about her actual problems, and now that Eliza was being so blatantly honest, Jan felt grateful for her company. The flicker of jealousy she'd felt was truly idiotic. Eliza was a real person in her life. Roberto was someone she was hot for for no real reason.

"So, what are you doing for Thanksgiving?" Jan asked. "Are you going back to Montana or what?"

"Are you kidding? My parents would have to kill a hog to fly me home. I'll probably have to pay my own way if I even go home in the summer, which I probably won't. I want to get one of those internships in New York—at some magazine maybe."

"I bet my mom could help you with that," Jan said.

Suddenly, the idea of going home for Thanksgiving with only her mother and her bickering sisters seemed claustrophobic. Adam had always been around on holidays—and this year he wouldn't be. Andy Berg had her own family to go to. And it didn't seem like Dad was going to make it back from Hong Kong. Anyway, where would he be staying if he did? Dad had no current home in the city, in the country, even. She definitely needed some buffer between herself and her family. Suddenly, the idea of inviting Eliza to spend Thanksgiving with her and her mother and sisters in New York seemed like an excellent idea—they'd all need some comic relief, some distraction.

Then there was the issue of Melanie. Jan hadn't had a chance to talk privately with Melanie during Family Weekend. She hadn't been sure what to say to her. She only knew what Erika had told her, and Erika wasn't exactly reliable. But maybe if she and Eliza were both there, Melanie would speak up? Melanie had seemed to like Eliza. If something really had happened to Melanie at that party, well, who better to have around than someone like Eliza—someone who actually had training at the Women's Crisis Center? Someone who was a well-known campus feminist?

"So, Eliza, I was thinking about Thanksgiving. Maybe you want to come to our house? We could talk to my mom about that internship idea? She and Dad both know people at all kinds of magazines, not only fashion. We could hang with my sisters. Consume everything in sight?" Eliza had intimidated Jan for months. But now that Jan knew her, she appreciated her outgoingness. It was a wild ride hanging out with Eliza sometimes. But what else was college supposed to be?

Eliza gave Jan a surprisingly bright and girlish smile. "Dude. I have been waiting all my life for just such an invitation. New Yawk City," she said, "is this cowgirl's dream town. Maybe I'll even teach you Russell gals a thing or two about roasting the Turducken."

"Oh no, no, no," Jan said, laughing. "You're the guest. Mom'll put you on pie duty."

"That's all right," Eliza said. "I loves to gets my fingers in all sorts a pies."

Jan laughed, even though she wasn't sure exactly what Eliza meant by this. It sounded dirty, and Jan had a twinge of regret. Maybe her family wasn't ready for a visit from Eliza. But it was too late. She'd already invited her. Eliza was practically beaming as she texted her mother to tell her the news. "My moms was feeling kinda guilty for not sending me a plane ticket. Now I can tell her she can rest easy. She doesn't need to kill ol' Betty Blue to finance my turkey day."

17

Dear Ms. Jensen,

I am writing to ask for a meeting with you because there has been an incident involving an RD girl at a party. Please, can this be a completely confidential conversation? This incident involves drinking and a sexual encounter. Someone close to me needs help.

Sincerely,
Erika Russell

"Erika, why don't you tell your mom what you told me on Tuesday?" Ms. Jensen tilted her head and looked expectantly at Erika. Ms. Jensen was perky, with her short blond curls and bright brown eyes—probably still only in her twenties. Erika had been having weekly counseling sessions with Ms. Jensen since the fall of her freshman year. Before that, she saw Mr. Katz, in the lower school. For as long as she'd been in school, she'd been pulled out of class once a week for a session with a guidance counselor. Sometimes, there were monthly meetings where kids with "low social cognition" met in groups and discussed various difficulties they had at school, and how they had dealt with them.

Now, Erika was in the awkward situation of having to explain to Mom about what she had said to Ms. Jensen. Ms. Jensen said in this case she had no choice, what Erika was describing could have been an assault—a crime—and the guidance counselor had a professional obligation to report it. She could be fired if she failed to at least discuss the matter with a parent.

"Well, it was at that party, at James Jamison's on Halloween." Erika looked at Ms. Jensen, and Ms. Jensen leaned forward slightly, staring at Erika with her wide, watery eyes. "Everything was fine with us—I mean with Binky and Morris and me. None of that old crowd that wasn't nice to Binky from uptown was invited to the party. It was mostly really nice people. But, there was punch, and some people were smoking and I don't know. Other stuff. Everyone had some punch. You couldn't even taste the alcohol in it. It made it hard to concentrate. We were playing cards, and I stopped after only a couple sips, because it was poker, and I had to stay focused." Erika stopped and looked from her mother to Ms. Jensen. Neither of them seemed particularly surprised by the fact that she was admitting to having tasted the punch. She'd felt guilty the couple of times she'd had more than a sip or two of Morris's beer at a party. She knew her mom didn't want her to drink. Girls like her, her mother had warned, could get themselves in trouble. She was too pretty, her mom had cautioned, and too "inexperienced." Erika thought what her mom meant was that she was too stupid, too stupid when it came to things like boys and parties to complicate matters by drinking. She had been inclined to agree. The feeling of even a little alcohol made everything so confusing. It was confusing thinking back on that night at the party. Erika hadn't been drunk—far from it. But still, there had been a pleasant, almost musical flow to everything—until the moment she had opened the door to that room.

Ms. Jensen said nothing. She waited in that unnervingly patient way that therapists had. It reminded Erika of the way animals often froze when they heard a sound, staring at nothing, waiting for it to become something.

"Melanie was very drunk. We couldn't find her. Then, when we did, it was, well, she was undressed. She was undressed but only the lower part of her." Erika looked away.

She took a deep breath. There it was, the truth. Or at least, a part of the truth. You had to see a person like that—naked, unconscious, on a bear rug, in a strange house—for the feeling to descend like the worst sort of weather, like a tiny tornado in your brain. A black nothingness that sucked its own meaning right out of your head before you knew what to do. You could call it a name, though. Erika knew that now. That's what the slut walk had been about. You called it by its name and the dark nothingness, the tornado, could be stopped.

"She was raped. Melanie was raped at James Jamison's party." Erika exhaled. She glanced at her mother. Her mother's face was pale and still. Then her mother dropped her head and pressed her fingers into her forehead, as though rubbing away the words she had just heard.

"Did Melanie talk to you about what happened?" Ms. Jensen asked. "Did she say anything about a boy, about anything she remembered?"

"No. She really couldn't speak at all that night, and then whenever I said anything to her—well, I only tried to say something once—she was really angry."

"What did she do?" Julia asked.

"She said if I told anyone anything she'd kill me."

"Oh, for God's sake," Julia said. "I guess she wouldn't be worried about you saying anything if she wasn't pretty sure something happened. She's just trying to push whatever it was out of her mind, Erika. It's not about you."

"Right," agreed Ms. Jensen.

"I know," said Erika. "But I don't think she'll ever talk to me again if she finds out I said something."

"Well, you did the right thing," Ms. Jensen said. "Someday, Melanie will realize that."

Mom lifted her head and looked at Erika. Her look was sad, almost crumbling. Erika wondered whether Mom was disappointed in her for not keeping a better eye on Melanie. "Maybe I should have stayed closer to her at that party. I didn't know about the punch. I mean how drunk people were getting from it. Now, people are saying even worse stuff. Like a bunch of guys from uptown had these drugs, and that lots of girls got drugs in their drinks. But I don't think that's true. I didn't see anything else like that going on."

"I don't want you to think for a second that this is in any way your fault, Erika." Mom now seemed actually angry, though she was saying Erika wasn't to blame. Why, then, was she speaking so harshly to her? Erika felt her eyes fill with tears and her throat tighten.

She tried to remember what Ms. Jensen told her to do when she felt confused or upset with how someone was speaking to her. She counted in her head to five and thought of a calming image. She often thought of sassafras plants at times like this, because they had a nice smell, and odd, mismatched leaves. But now she found herself thinking of other things, like the freckle-nosed girl from Brown. She didn't think about the kiss the girl gave her, just the girl's bright eyes, and the way she had laughed about it all afterward. It was a laugh like chimes, like a xylophone. Erika liked that sound and wished her mother's voice rang with those high, light tones now. Thinking of that girl's voice seemed to help, at least for now, since Mom's brows were no longer coming together in a V and she was reaching out to pat her knee. Mom wasn't angry, Erika realized. She was upset.

"But you didn't see a boy leaving the room before you went in? There was no one with her during the party? One of the boys from uptown, maybe?" Ms. Jensen asked.

"I don't know who she spoke to at the party," Erika said. "The only boy we saw when we found her was Gerald. He was getting sick in the bathroom."

"Gerald?" Mom asked.

"Yeah, down the hallway near the room where we found Melanie, Gerald was in that part of the house in the bathroom."

"And were there other kids in that part of the house?" asked Ms. Jensen.

No, Erika explained, there hadn't been. That was why it had taken them a while to find Melanie. Most of the crowd was in the kitchen, where the punch and beer were, or dancing in the living room. The room Melanie was in was undisturbed. It had felt like maybe it was supposed to be off-limits to the partygoers.

"Well," Mom said, and sighed. "That would explain why she hasn't been hanging around after school. For weeks she's been coming straight home. I haven't heard her mention Gerald once."

"And that's unusual?" Ms. Jensen asked. The room felt tense, and Erika now felt a part of that tension—the feeling of her mother's emotions being directed at her had left her. Now, it was like the three of them were working together, solving the mystery: it was Gerald. Of course, that much she already knew, had already discussed with Morris and Binky. But the adults had to reach the conclusion on their own. She'd had to guide them to it, but the conclusion was theirs.

"Will Gerald be arrested?" Erika asked, and suddenly all eyes were on her. She could feel her mother's emotions radiating out toward her again, only this time Ms. Jensen was also staring hard at her. At first, no one spoke.

"I don't think that needs to be the next step," Ms. Jensen said. "We really don't know what happened, no one knows, until Melanie can say. And it does seem like Melanie was very drunk. That complicates things a bit."

Erika noticed then, to her horror, that her mother had started to cry—not noisily, but tears appeared on her cheeks and her eyes were red-rimmed. What had she done? Now, even Mom seemed more confused than helpful. She'd risked Melanie's fury, and yet nothing, it seemed, was going to be done to solve the problem, to make it clear what had happened, to punish the wrongdoer. She wished her loud, blustery father were here. The situation, Erika began to think, called for someone who didn't care about either anger or tears, just the truth. "Maybe you should talk to Dad," Erika said, feeling that finally, perhaps, she'd said the right thing, had led them toward a worthwhile conclusion.

But Mom stood up and put her sunglasses on, speaking softly to Ms. Jensen. "I think," she said flatly, "it's time for me to have a talk with Melanie."

18

The boy in the dream had a triangular-shaped torso, with very broad shoulders and a trim, flat waist. She couldn't recall his face, but she knew, even when she was dreaming, that she did not know him. She placed her hands around his back and he pulled her into an embrace. She could feel the texture of his jersey—a silky green football shirt—and she enjoyed the feel of that cool, slippery fabric against her bare skin. Why, she recalled thinking, can I feel this real shirt, if this is only a dream? Then, she was kissing him, tilting her head back until it ached, because he was so tall. There was something gentle yet formidable about this dream boy; he was too tall for her, but he bent down deliberately and sweetly, to touch her. She felt a deep yearning for him, and at the same time that she recognized her own desire, the boy's face morphed into recognizable form. She began to smile at him. He was so goofy, and so tender—it was absurd that Edward would be this way.

She woke to a feeling of embarrassment and disappointment, a lonesome ache in her loins. She often had dreams from which she was disappointed to wake. But this one was different. The boy was clearly Edward merged with Gerald from the night he wore his football jersey to the party. Her own mind was taunting her. "Fuck," Melanie muttered. She hit the snooze button hard. She hit it hard enough that the little plastic button felt loose under her finger.

"Damn," she said to no one. "Goddamn."

It was Saturday, and she'd forgotten to turn off the stupid alarm, and now she'd squandered the opportunity to sleep in. Anyway, she was too agitated by the thought of dreaming about Edward/Gerald to find any temptation in rolling over and going back to sleep.

Melanie pulled on a pair of sweatpants, a hoodie, and her Tom's slip-ons. She loved padding around on a Saturday morning in her pajamas, not calling or texting anyone, not bothering with her hair, which stuck up at odd angles. Usually, she liked to get Julia to buy her something to eat from the farmers' market—cider doughnuts, or fresh eggs, which tasted so much better in an omelet—but she was barely speaking to her mom. She was definitely not talking to Erika. The question was not how to get through the next year and a half, until Erika went to college, having nothing whatsoever to do with her stupid sister; it was how to somehow slip away from Mom's sudden, exhausting scrutiny.

Melanie's entire life was about damage control.

It was bad enough that people had seen Mom at school, being escorted back to Ms. Jensen's office. What was worse was that Ms. Jensen herself had walked into tenth grade English lit and tapped Gerald on the shoulder, requesting that he come with her. Melanie had felt her face redden. Later, she'd heard from Jess that a few of the guys—Gerald's friends, guys from the basketball team—had begun to refer to this incident as Gerald's "perp walk." Gerald, the dumbass, had evidently told someone what had happened and now the news was spreading. There had been gossip right from the beginning about the party, of course, but the tide had now turned against Gerald.

New York City private school kids traveled in a tight circle. There were kids who knew other kids from Hebrew school, church groups, community service programs, summer camp, hockey, and soccer. A junior girl had asked Jess how she could hang out with someone like Gerald. When Jess had asked what she meant, the girl had lowered her voice. "You know," the girl said. "A perv like him. Aren't you afraid he'll slip something in your drink, too?" Jess had told the girl off, but it was no use. Everyone was saying the same thing—that Gerald had gotten his hands on some date-rape drug and had used it on his friend, Melanie. There were even rumors about where he had gotten it, and how some people had seen guys who were clearly plain-clothes officers down by the river where lots of people bought drugs. It didn't matter if this were true or not. Everything any-one saw now became part of the story—her story.

That tap on the shoulder from Ms. Jensen was the end—it

had turned the crisis, at least publicly, from Melanie's crisis to Gerald's. She recalled how Gerald had glanced her way. How his mouth had twisted like a little kid's who was trying not to cry. Melanie had shaken her head "no," as he glanced back at her, but she wasn't sure he'd seen her. Why would he ever think she'd say anything to Ms. Jensen? How ridiculous was that? It was just how the gossip had flowed—at first there had been the post tagging Melanie as a drunk hoe, but then something else had gotten started. It wasn't about the people in the story anymore. It was about whoever was telling the story.

"Good morning, sweetie." Mom looked up from her computer. She was typing furiously when Mel walked in, so she must have been working, which was a good sign. It was good to see her mother preoccupied with her own life.

"Do you want to take a walk? Go get some breakfast? Erika's still sleeping. I think she was up late playing that game of hers, so if you want just the two of us could slip over to Trina's." Julia spoke without looking up from her computer screen.

Trina's was the bakery/cafe that was the rage in Tribeca for brunch. But it was actually early enough for the two of them to get a table. Despite Melanie's reluctance to be alone with her mother, the idea of sneaking out on Erika and getting a delicious basket of warm croissants was tempting. The idea of buttery bread gave her a slight lurching feeling in her stomach—she was really starving. "Sure, but I'm going like this, if that's okay." There was no point in wearing a cool outfit to go to Trina's with her mother.

"Of course!" Julia stood up so quickly from her work, Melanie almost regretted her decision—Mom definitely seemed to still be in near-panic mode, judging by how quickly she'd seized on the opportunity to get her alone. She wasn't sure why, if Mom thought what had happened to her at James Jamison's Halloween party had shattered her entire existence, a basket of warm bread would be particularly beneficial, but at least going to Trina's wouldn't totally suck.

Mom scrawled a note to Erika, promising to bring her back her favorite scones and jam, and the two of them left with Maxwell scratching and whining at the door behind them.

"He knows it's not a school day and he thinks he should be coming," Melanie said.

"Well, if I ever start bringing my dog in a purse to Trina's you have my permission, Melanie, to shoot me in the head." Melanie laughed. It'd be fun, actually, to bring Maxwell to Trina's, but she could see why Mom would hate herself for being that type. Mom was always saying stuff like that, like if she started wearing pants that fell so low they showed her butt, that she should shoot her in the head and put her out of her misery. Melanie always thought that was an exceptionally unmotherly sort of thing to say.

It was a beautiful morning and they had to weave through the early crowd at the farmers' market to work their way up Greenwich Street. Why, Melanie wondered, were people always killing themselves in Tribeca to be first in line for everything? First in line for hot cider, for a basket of pears? But fortunately,

Mom didn't stop to talk to anyone. Mom knew half the world, and she'd even talk to the other half if they happened to be in line for something ahead of her.

Then just as they were walking into Trina's, Julia suddenly stopped in her tracks. A strange man who was exiting Trina's on the opposite side of the steps grabbed Julia's arm. "Hey, you!" he said. "I almost didn't recognize you without the pooch!" The guy had thin silverish hair and wore a sort of string bracelet, the kind that was supposed to signify something—serenity, Buddha, yoga. He didn't look gay, though, like some guys who wore jewelry. He had on jeans and a loose flannel shirt that was untucked. He carried an iPad under his arm, which he patted as he spoke to Julia. "Funny to see you, actually, I was just reading your column!"

"Really?" Julia seemed truly surprised, and Melanie began to get an unsettled feeling about him—why would some random guy be reading her mother's column? Who was this guy? "Yeah, my sister's big five-oh is this week and I thought I'd check out available advice on what to get a woman for her fiftieth. I liked your idea about the movie library—though I'd quibble over some of your suggestions. I mean, *Thelma and Louise*—seriously?"

Melanie looked at her mother, waiting for some sort of explanation, but Julia was blushing and chuckling like a schoolgirl. "Oh, well, that's the beauty of the idea—you get whatever movie classics work for you—the point is to get a lot of them, so it's like a real library. And to get things you know the other person wouldn't necessarily buy, but they'd watch. You know. Like *Saturday Night Fever*. Something that induces shame."

Induces shame? That was the flippant way Julia spoke at home, to them, to Dad, not the way she spoke to men Melanie didn't even know. Her parents had been separated just since the summer, only a few months. Could her mother possibly have begun dating? The idea actually made her want to cry, in the way that a childlike sob would sometimes catch in her throat unexpectedly, a force within her that was almost alien, decidedly out of her own control. Melanie put her hand on Julia's forearm. "Come on, I'm starving." She practically had to pull her mother into the restaurant. Mom turned around and looked at Melanie with a faint air of surprise. It was as if for just a second, in spite of all the drama going on with her, Mom had forgotten Melanie even existed.

"So what was that all about?" Melanie had wolfed down her first croissant and was starting to feel calm again. Trina's was large, with lots of small tables on one side, and then another side with big soft banquettes. It was early enough for them to have been seated on one of those plush banquettes, even though it was just the two of them. Waitresses walked by in Trina's trademark blue button-down shirts with crisp white aprons. Everyone who worked there looked to Melanie like they were born in Vermont or Wisconsin—someplace where people still milked cows with buckets and learned to knit or weave.

"Oh, his name's Scott. I met him at the dog run." Julia leaned over and took a sip of her latte. She still had color in her cheeks—either from the cool air, or her excitement at running into Scott. She looked younger again, strikingly different than she had only an hour before when hunched over her laptop. But she didn't look young in a good way; she looked young, perhaps, because she was seeming a little foolish.

"Did you go out with him?" Melanie asked, her voice catching. She hadn't intended to be so forthright; the question seemed to pop out fully formed.

"Out?" Julia asked. "Oh, I wasn't out with him." She laughed in a way that made Melanie feel transparent, and small. "We ran into each other with the dogs by the Latin café—actually on Halloween—and we sat down and had a drink. . . ." Julia's voice trailed off. That had been the night of Melanie's disaster, and she could see in her mother's face that, as she spoke, she recognized the fact that while she, Julia, newly single, and perhaps eager to meet someone new, drank wine with this strange man, she had been at James Jamison's now infamous party, a few miles away.

Everyone close to Melanie was acting as if they knew what had happened that night, better than she did. Now here was her own mother, half admitting to having her own secrets, perhaps covering her own tracks. There was no way she was opening up to her now. It was somehow more impossible than ever. Her mother was like a girl, just another overeager girl, at least where boys and men were concerned. Blushing and lying like she was, she seemed untrustworthy. Melanie yearned suddenly for her father, for his stupid no-nonsense ways, for her parents' old marriage, which had kept them so preoccupied with each other's faults it had shielded her from parental probing.

Anyway, it was only Gerald who could really say what had happened, and she had refused to talk to Gerald. She had refused even when Ms. Jensen and her mother pleaded with her. She had refused when that pudgy little therapist her mother sent her to, Pat Landau, pursed her lips together and cocked her head and asked, "But weren't you and the boy in question friends?"

Since the perp walk, she doubted Gerald would talk to her. What could she do about the fact that other girls had claimed Gerald had tried to give them drinks that tasted odd—sodas from the soda machine in the cafeteria, as if that made any sense at all? A friend of Lani Elliot's, Susan Somebody, had even spit on Gerald in the stairwell. Jess had seen it herself, and other kids had laughed, while Gerald turned beet red and wiped the top of his head with his shirt sleeve. Louis Finke had been there too, Jess said. He'd called out, "Yo, these bitches are out of control," and Ms. Regelman, the assistant principal, had been down the hall, and had called Louis over to her. Jess didn't know what happened with Louis, but he didn't show up in math until half-way through the period, and he didn't look happy.

It was like the whole grade was at war, boys against girls. But it wasn't Melanie's fault. There wasn't anything she could have done to stop her idiot sister from blabbing. Anyway, she wasn't even friends with Lani and her crowd of followers. Those girls were about the drama, and drama was the last thing Melanie was looking for at school. Still, she wondered if Susan would get in trouble for spitting, or if Ms. Regelman was maybe taking the side of the girls. She wondered when the whole thing would end. When would people move on?

Julia put down her coffee cup and eyed Melanie. "I'm sorry, sweetheart," she said.

"Sorry for what?" Melanie asked, wondering what her mother might know about the absurd situation she was in at school—how she half wanted to defend Gerald about the dumbest accusations, just to get everything back to normal, or at least back to where she could control her own stupid story.

"Sorry I wasn't focused on you enough? I mean, maybe I needed to focus on you, not Erika. I always worry about her."

"Why? Because she's too pretty?" Melanie let the word *pretty* hang in the air between them. Of course she was pretty, too, but she wasn't Erika-pretty. "And dumb," Melanie added. The word sounded absurdly childish even to her, and she half regretted saying it, but then Julia clicked her tongue and looked away. Her expression of helplessness gave Melanie a sudden chill.

"I wish you two could watch out for each other. But I guess it's not fair to expect that."

"You mean it's not fair to expect me to be like Jan?"

The waitress returned to the table and placed Melanie's poached egg in front of her. Melanie dove into her breakfast.

"I don't expect you to be like Jan, but I don't like the way you push Erika away all the time. I know she isn't exactly *cool*, but she cares about you more than you know. Anyway, I know you're both disoriented without Dad here, and that's exacerbating the issue." Her mother's mouth quivered in the way that made Melanie at once furious and uneasy. Why couldn't her mother pull herself together? She didn't blame her mother for her father's leaving, and she hated it when her mother seemed to blame herself. She hated that her mother seemed to be moving on, interested in other guys, even lame-looking ones, who wore stupid, trendy man-bracelets. It made it seem like everything, their whole family, Melanie's existence, was part of a huge mistake.

Melanie sighed. She knew Erika cared. In fact she cared too much. She was always getting in her business, like the time she took it upon herself to report to their parents that she had been smoking cigarettes, when she'd taken a few puffs off a tangerine-mint-flavored electronic cigarette. Erika had claimed she was concerned about Melanie's health, but Melanie knew that wasn't the case. Erika just needed to stick her nose where it didn't belong. All this crap about showing her concern for Melanie was really a way for Erika to appear superior, a way for her to be like Jan, to seem like the new oldest. "I don't want to talk about it," Melanie said, her mouth full.

Julia buried her face in her coffee cup. It seemed like Melanie, with her prickliness, had won this round. Ever since Mom had found out about "the incident," Mom had been easier on her. She'd taken her word for it that she didn't need any tests for STDs. Melanie had known Gerald since forever and knew for a fact he'd had zero real experience with girls. In the meeting with Ms. Jensen, Mom even said that, at least for now, she wasn't going to mention the whole thing to Dad. She had said something about it being a "women's issue" and that maybe when and if she was ready they could talk to her father, and consider the part her drinking had played in it all, but for now Mom seemed to think that Melanie needed time to "heal," and Ms. Jensen agreed, and then sent her off to pudgy Pat Landau.

Pat Landau had said healing takes time, and she'd explained about trauma, and she even asked Melanie to whack the back of a chair with a stuffed sock, and said that she could visualize Gerald when she was hitting the chair, if that helped. She could visualize whatever made her angriest. But all Melanie could see was Pat Landau, the chair, and the sock, all of which made her angry enough to whack the red metal chair back ten or fifteen times with all her strength. She hated the chair for being one of those school-building chairs you never saw anywhere else. She hated the sock for being a sock, a stupid, stupid prop in a therapy ritual that didn't help her heal at all, only humiliated her further, since only a total idiot would spend her time whacking chairs and talking to sympathetic, dough-faced therapists.

If everyone at school would get out of her life, she'd heal just fine. She thought of Jan and Eliza and how they had talked about frat guys at Brown, and boys in high school.

Maybe what they said about what boys wanted was true. But if it was, what did girls actually want? What had she wanted on the balcony with the good-looking pirate boy who'd laughed at her?

Melanie suddenly felt stuffed. Mom bent over and got her purse and picked up the bag of Erika's scones. Melanie knew she'd been irritable with her mother, but this time she didn't regret it. Mom had pretty much admitted to favoring Erika. Anyway, what was she doing with this whole Scott thing? Why would she want to get a drink with a guy like that? That he had a dog with him was a lame excuse. The whole story made Mom seem a little sad. A little sad and maybe kind of pathetic since Dad was gone. Mom was too old to go chasing after guys like that, guys she knew nothing about, who wore jewelry, who were absolutely nothing like her father.

———

When Melanie and Julia got back home, Erika was doing a yoga video in the living room. "Oh, I just started this—anyone want to join me?" Erika didn't get out of her deep, wobbly lunge, and the sight of her sister straining to hold such a basic pose filled Melanie with contempt.

"Oh, I'll give it a try, although I'm so full I think I'll burst," Mom said, and Erika paused the video to wait for Julia to change. Melanie stared hard at Erika, who stood alone in the living room in her yoga pants and a gray T-shirt. She wasn't wearing a bra, but she had the kind of long, sinewy figure that looked great au natural. She had her hair pulled up on top of her head, showing the full length of her golden-brown neck and her improbably tiny ears. Erika wasn't pretty. She was extraordinary, like some sort of animal, filled with a natural grace. Melanie twirled a strand of hair and tried to feel something other than a pure hatred of her sister, but nothing was there. She couldn't do it for Mom. She couldn't do it to keep the peace now that it was only the three of them at home.

If only Erika had been a normal girl none of this would be happening. The Halloween party would be something Melanie might talk to Jess about once or twice, but it would be her secret to do with what she wanted. Now she was "the girl who . . ." and she'd never live it down, even with her own family. Now Gerald was lost to her—not that he'd ever been so important, but did he really deserve to have everyone in school calling him horrible things? Spitting and jeering at him? But even if he did deserve it, it didn't help Melanie put the whole thing behind her. It sucked to have a sister like Erika. It sucked to live with a clueless, tattle-tale genius. It sucked to have a sister everyone would die to look like, but no one would ever want to be.

Melanie went to her room and shut the door. She didn't open her computer or check her phone, her usual first reflexes whenever she got home. Instead she lay on her bed and looked at the ceiling. There was nothing to be done about the situation at school. What could she say to a bunch of whispering idiots? They'd talk as long as they wanted. Everyone at RD loved drama. Calling Gerald a perv made them all feel righteous. Pitying her gave them some sort of thrill, too. She was like a girl in a book or a magazine or one of Ms. Jensen's inane scenarios from Adolescent Issues. She was the girl for whom all of that well-meaning adolescent advice came too late. Therapy might allow her to talk about her problems, but it didn't allow her to fix them. There had to be something she could do.

t was mid-November—the best time of year to be in the Berkshires. The leaves had mostly fallen and made great mounds on either end of the yard that Gerald and Edward had been forced to rake. Gerald still had the blisters on his hands from the weekend before to prove it. But now were the tasks he'd come to enjoy—the wood-splitting and the burning of debris. Their father had taught them how to do both of these tasks over the last ten years. When the boys were younger— Gerald ten and Edward thirteen—their father had shown them how to clear the area around the brush, removing anything that might burn; how to feed the fire the larger branches and leaves first; and how to tamp the leaves down so the burning leaves wouldn't be caught in the wind and become airborne fire starters. He'd taught them how to split wood, not because they couldn't buy all they needed right down the road at Coleman's shop, but because it was something a guy ought to know how to do. Gerald liked the way the ax felt in his hand. Even more, he liked to use the chain saw with his dad, liked how the saw's vibrations ran up his arms and through his chest.

Now, it was Edward who was working at the edge of the yard battling back the saplings that encroached too far into the grass for his liking. Gerald was readying the leaves for burning. He was carefully pushing the leaves down beneath the larger branches he and Edward had gathered from the property—branches that had fallen last year during the ice storms and nor'easters—branches that had snapped off in the wind, branches they had been lucky hadn't fallen on the house.

Gerald had always thought of their city apartment as his mother's and the country home as his father's, although, naturally, they each owned them both. The Berkshire house, however, had been Gerald's father's family home for at least three generations. At some point, it had been operated as an inn, and it felt that way inside—a rambling place with no real center to it. Once when he was a little boy, Gerald hid on the third floor below the rafters where his mother hung her old clothes, and it had taken the family almost a full hour to find him, although it had occurred to Gerald since then that, perhaps, no one had actually been looking for him.

Gerald never forgot for a single moment that his father was dead. His absence stood in contrast to everything he saw, everything he felt. But at the house, his father's absence was so thick, so impossible to navigate, that he had given up trying and simply lived there with his ghost. If he cut wood with Edward, the nearness of his father's image was with him. If he walked down the road to the store, there was his father, buying the *New York Times*. If he drove with Edward into town, or snuck a beer from the fridge, always, there was his father, neither approving nor disapproving, but felt as an ever-receding outline. Someone he still longed for, if only to say good-bye.

Gerald's father had died the summer Gerald turned twelve. It had been only that spring that his father had begun throwing up blood, so that his mother had taken him to the emergency room. After that, he'd been home only for a few weeks. It had been stomach cancer. It had taken his father without anyone even noticing. Sometimes Gerald wondered what would have happened if one of them had been paying closer attention—if they had caught on to the symptoms a few months, or even weeks earlier. Sometimes he blamed Edward, who was the oldest, and the closest to their father. Sometimes he blamed his mother, who knew everything about him. Often, he blamed himself. He was the quiet, less athletic boy. He didn't have as much to do as Edward, who played three sports to his one. With all that time Gerald spent messing around in his room, playing video games, you'd think he would have had the time to notice that his father was dying.

Now, whenever they went to the country, which was most weekends, Edward and Gerald did chores, things their father had always done. They cleaned gutters, and did the yard work. They picked out a new grill. They called the guys to come and remove the old furnace and install a new one. They did these things because their mother was alone. She worked hard all week as an attorney at a midtown firm. She paid their way, along with Dad's life insurance, for everything they needed. But she wasn't a strong woman. After their father died, she worked all day, then came home and cooked, and then she drank. Gerald didn't know how much she drank. He didn't think she was an alcoholic. But she drank the way some women read or did yoga, as a pastime, as a way to stave off boredom. She was bored with her husband gone, and just the kids to care for. She was bored with her life, and Gerald was afraid of what would happen when she finally realized she didn't want to drink a bottle of pinot noir each night in front of the TV. He worried that she'd no longer have other options.

———

What was different about gathering the yard debris and lighting the fire this time was that Gerald was not content to simply do these things side by side with Edward, each of them working on their own separate tasks until their bodies ached with fatigue. What was different was that Gerald wanted to talk. What was different was that Gerald was so tired of his loneliness, his pariah-like status at school, he'd given in and let the words tumble out.

It wasn't until he had asked his question, and stood to throw a last branch on the fire, that it occurred to Gerald that talking to Edward might be a mistake. Edward had displayed an almost brotherly affection toward Melanie Russell for years. Gerald hadn't missed that Melanie seemed to flirt with Edward and was more inclined to hang around at his house when his brother was home. Gerald had often felt jealous of Edward and annoyed by the way Melanie seemed to hang on his every word. Edward was tall and muscular. He ran winter track and was, without question, the reason Rose Dyer made it to the Independent Schools final conference.

Edward was on Gerald so quickly, at first Gerald thought he'd been hit not by his brother's fist, but by a branch that had somehow become dislodged from the brush fire. He thought he had somehow caught fire, the pain in his jaw was so intense.

The question Gerald asked had touched a nerve. He had begun hesitantly, but then blurted the end out all at once. Had he, Edward, ever, you know, messed around with a girl when maybe he shouldn't have—when maybe they were both too drunk? It was something Gerald needed to know. He needed to know whether what he had done had been done by other boys, by other men, who were not criminals—who might even be in love with a girl. He wanted to know if it was possible to do something, and to know that it was wrong at the time, but still not be completely at fault. Could drunkenness absolve you of having made a bad, albeit somewhat conscious, decision? Was there something so terrible in what he had done, when he had wanted Melanie Russell for so long, and then she had come to him, so sweetly, so yieldingly, floating on a stream, as it seemed at the time, of rum-spiked punch?

The blow that landed on Gerald's jaw was a response to this question. So was Edward's glowering face that appeared unnaturally contorted over the flames of their bonfire. The ringing in his ears was too loud for Gerald to take in what Edward was saying, but he heard the words "motherfucker" and "loser." Then he heard something about frying his balls in the bonfire. But that couldn't be right. Edward had already been walking away. What he'd heard might have just been the wind, or the crackling of the leaves and wood. When he got to his feet, Gerald's shirt smelled like smoke, and he could taste blood in his mouth. He felt, however, somehow cleansed. He knew now for certain what he'd suspected for the last two weeks at school. That in the eyes of the entire world, he was a piece of shit.

20

The clock said six o'clock. Melanie's first reaction was to roll over and go back to sleep. She usually didn't get up until at least six thirty, sometimes seven. But then she realized something was wrong. She was in her clothes and her watch was still on her wrist. Out the window, the sun was beginning to set over the Hudson. Melanie had the vague recollection of her mother coming into her room and touching her on the forehead, just as she drifted off to sleep. She recalled feeling her mother's gaze—her breath as she stood over her, as if waiting for her to wake. Melanie had half wanted to get up, but the effort required to rouse herself from sleep was too great, and she let sleep take her under, like the pull of a wave.

Now it was six in the evening, and she was groggy. She could hear voices in the kitchen—it was Erika and Jan and Eliza. They must have gotten back from shopping. Jan and Eliza were lucky. They were done with the whole vomit bowl of high school—off in college—free—Melanie couldn't wait for the day.

She listened to their voices. They were unpacking the groceries they had gotten for Mom, since Mom had to go uptown to meet with her editor, Dana, at *Candy*. Melanie had told the others that she had work to get out of the way before the holiday and couldn't help them shop for Thanksgiving, but that was a partial truth. What work she had could be knocked off in an hour. She simply didn't want to go along with the rest of them. She had been avoiding Erika every chance she could, and she wasn't about to change her policy. Her fury at Erika was so intense it was almost a pleasure. When looking at Erika, she could feel her lips curl in a distaste that was almost a smile. She hated the way Erika wore her hair in a too-high ponytail. She hated the purple Converse sneakers she wore with everything. She hated above all the almost unnatural smoothness of Erika's skin. She looked like a doll. But a huge doll. A huge ungraceful doll in a constant state of surprise. Whenever Erika wasn't surprised, she was sad or hurt. Just this morning, Melanie had told Erika to go to school without her and Erika opened her mouth and stared at her like a fish. "Why?" she choked out.

"I'm changing—I'm not ready," Melanie had answered and had retreated into the bedroom. She had found some excuse or another every day to leave either before Erika or after her. Occasionally, if they left at the same time, Melanie stopped off in the bodega for a soda or gum. She'd dart in at the last minute, leaving Erika either to follow foolishly, or walking along the street not even realizing, until it was too late, that her sister had bailed on her yet again.

But Erika hadn't asked this morning why Melanie wasn't ready. She'd asked a different question.

"Why do you hate me?" Erika had asked. "Why do you hate me so much?" She stood there with tears in her eyes, with her book bag on her back, looking like an enormous toddler.

"I don't," Melanie had finally answered. "I just want you to leave me alone. I want you to stay the fuck out of my life." She wanted Erika neutralized. She wanted Erika to shut up. She wanted Erika to stop looking at her, waiting for her. She wanted Erika to stop.

Earlier, before she retreated to her room, Melanie had been staring out the window wondering how long it would take Jan to figure out something was going on—or how long it would take Mom to spill the beans to Jan and bring her into the big mess with Gerald, assuming she hadn't already. That was when Melanie noticed Mom down at the dog run.

The dog run was half a block away, and the apartment was on the twenty-fifth floor, so Melanie's view was perfectly clear. Mom sat on the little dogs' side of the dog park, and she was sitting, quite close, to a man. It was Scott, the guy from Trina's with the bracelet. Mom really did hang out with that guy.

Melanie watched from the window, hoping her mother would get up and leave or talk to someone else, but she and Scott seemed to keep to themselves. Mom even threw her head back in laughter once or twice, and reached out, she thought, to touch Scott's arm. Her mother was being a total idiot.

"Let me have that," Jan said. "I have got to have one of those stuffed pepper things in the next five seconds. You have no idea how disgusting the food is at school. We're subsisting entirely on BLTs."

"Mom said those are for tomorrow," Erika said.

Back in her bed, Melanie could hear the girls' voices from the kitchen. Jan's voice familiar, yet strange to hear at home after so many months. She had only caught a glimpse of Eliza when the girls arrived in the afternoon. She wore suspenders and a skirt with Doc Martens and tights with big yellow flowers on them. Her hair, Melanie thought, was a darker red, and it had grown out slightly on the side, and looked more like normal hair.

When Eliza walked into the Russells' apartment, she'd said, "Well, well, so this is how the other half lives." At first, Melanie didn't know which half Eliza was talking about. But then Eliza went on. "I think my whole house could fit in this one apartment. This place is like three double-wides." Melanie laughed because their apartment was nothing special compared to how her friends lived. There'd been times when Melanie had gone to someone's house and had wanted to make a similar comment, but held her tongue. But what was so bad about saying what you thought? She got up from her bed. Maybe Eliza was enough of a distraction that she could cope with being around the rest of her loser family.

She thought maybe she would tell Jan about Mom and

that guy Scott. Maybe Jan was in the know. Mom sometimes confided in Jan, because Jan was the oldest. But that would probably make things worse. Jan might dismiss the whole thing as silly, or she'd get upset herself that Mom was so desperate she'd look twice at a guy like that. Still, seeing Mom down there with Scott gave Melanie a strange feeling—a tingling sensation that reached all the way down her back. Maybe she was actually sick—feverish? She couldn't tell sometimes whether she was physically ill or just upset. She never seemed to be only a little upset anymore, in the way that allowed her to tell what the source of her distress might be. These days, her emotions simply overtook her entire body. She never felt like talking to anyone, even Jess, who was the last person to judge anyone for being a drama queen. She couldn't talk. The only thing that brought her back to normal was doing simple things—checking her email, taking a shower, getting a snack. She forced herself out of bed and into the kitchen to see Jan. A normal person would go into the kitchen, she told herself.

Erika, Jan, and Eliza were all still unpacking the food. There must have been ten bags of stuff, with nowhere to put half of it. There was the turkey Mom ordered—it was enormous and took up almost a whole shelf in the fridge. The three of them were pulling out all the old, regular food—yogurt, leftover pasta, cottage cheese—and piling it on the counter. Melanie grabbed a yogurt and pulled the top off. "What are you doing with all this stuff?"

"I haven't got the slightest idea." Jan laughed. "I just know it can't stay in here. Maybe we'll have some of it for dinner."

"This is like a week's worth of food in my house," Eliza said. "I mean, this yogurt—this Greek shit? Do you know what it costs? My mom would lose it on me if I brought that home. If I were all vegetarian, like Erika here, I'd be living on cornflakes, I guess. Anyway, you can't be a vegetarian where I come from. You know what we call the cows, back where I live? They're called 'beefs,' 'cause that's what they are. Food. Walking food."

Erika made a face, and Melanie laughed. Eliza was too much for Erika—too in-your-face. That kind of girl really rattled Erika's nerves.

"Yeah, I don't know what Erika's eating—that Tofurkey crap? What is in there? How do you know they're not sneaking in like little tiny particles of turkey brain, or some other part they can't sell to regular people?"

Erika rolled her eyes. "They have quality controls, Melanie. It's all processed and checked by food-manufacturing experts. It's actually interesting scientifically—how they reproduce molecules that mimic the way certain animal proteins, certain amino acids, react with taste receptors."

"Who the fuck *are* you?" Eliza asked. "You're like Madame Russell-Curie."

Melanie laughed, her mouth full of yogurt. "That's just the beginning. Now she'll get on a roll and we'll start hearing about why eating meat can cause kidney disease, and blah, blah."

Erika stopped placing the brussels sprouts in the fridge and turned around to look at Melanie. "I would never say that," she said, a look of hurt crossing her face. "That's not even true—I mean there's no basis in fact for that at all." It wasn't Melanie's taunting that had upset Erika. It was the randomness of the accusation.

"You little Russell chicklets ought to chill out. It's like one false move around here and the kitchen is going to combust." Eliza said.

"Yeah," Jan said, suddenly reclaiming her older-sister position. "Let's just get this crap put away and find something in here worth eating. Mom said we should do whatever we want—she isn't going to be home until ten or so. She said she invited her editor friend to come tomorrow and we aren't eating until pretty late—so none of that prep stuff she asked us to do really has to happen tonight. You guys want to go see a movie with us?"

"Well, Jan, in my inventory-taking of your family cupboards, I have assessed that there is simply too much booze in this house for your mom to notice what might be missing," Eliza said. "What is this, like two cases of wine? Perhaps the movie can wait until post-zinfandel?"

"Mom belongs to some wine-of-the-month club, and they send stuff she doesn't like, so it piles up," Jan said.

"Well, is she the type to keep track of the shit she doesn't imbibe?"

"Mom is pretty chill about that. She'll let us have wine at dinner. Don't know about Melanie, though. Does Mom let you have wine yet, Mel?"

Mel shrugged. Her mother had been letting her occasionally have a glass of wine at dinner on the weekend, but she wasn't sure about now, since the PTs concert and the Gerald nightmare, thanks to Erika's big mouth. "Sometimes," she answered uncertainly.

"I think this lovely, what is it—a California zin, plenty of berry flavor, hint of cherry?—this would be a fine accompaniment to our—what are we having?"

"It looks like pasta with mushrooms and prosciutto," Jan said, peering into a plastic container.

"Excellent," replied Eliza as she scrounged through the drawer looking for a corkscrew. "And fortunately, there are two bottles of this same shit. We won't even require fresh glassware." Eliza was prancing around the kitchen in her flowered stockings, twirling ballerina-like with Mom's best wineglasses.

———

Melanie got out the place mats and started to set the dining room table for the four of them. She liked the idea of staying in with Jan and Eliza. Maybe Erika would get uncomfortable enough to leave them all alone. The girls found more leftovers from the week, microwaved them, and tossed them onto plates—there was broccoli, some sort of turkey chili Mom made on Monday, and pad thai they'd ordered in yesterday. Eliza came to the table carrying the wineglasses, and Jan brought out the first bottle of wine. Jan was definitely giving Melanie permission to join the party. Melanie had suspected Mom had told Jan about the Halloween disaster, but if she had, Jan was being cool about it. She wasn't pressing her for information or acting like she was some sort of terrible person.

The first taste of wine on her tongue had a familiar sourness. Her mother's philosophy was that the girls should learn from adults what moderate drinking was like. She let them try different wines and explained about varieties of grapes and how wine could be dry or sweet. But those lessons hadn't helped her much at the party. The punch had been so sweet she couldn't even taste the alcohol in it, which must have been something really strong. She hadn't gotten out of control at the Thongs concert, the way Jess had. She had been careful and had paced herself.

"So how's everything been around here with Dad gone?" Jan asked. They had eaten most everything on the table, with Eliza scarfing her food down so fast Melanie had to wonder if she was the type who'd be on her way to the bathroom any second to puke it up. They had polished off the first bottle of wine between the three of them—Erika wasn't drinking, and Jan had gotten up to open another bottle. Melanie wasn't drunk, though, just warm and relaxed.

"I think Mom's acting kind of weird," Melanie said. Erika shot her a look from across the table. Erika had started emailing someone from her iPad, but she was, annoyingly, still hanging out at the table with them, watching Eliza like she was some sort of celebrity—someone notorious and glamorous. Melanie found having Eliza in the apartment an exciting diversion, too, but she wasn't staring at the girl like she was an alien life-form.

"What do you mean weird?" Jan asked.

"Well . . ." Melanie hesitated. "There's this guy." A hush fell around the table as Melanie recounted how she and Mom had run into Scott at Trina's and then how she'd seen Mom just a few hours earlier hanging out with the same guy at the dog run.

Jan shook her head. "I don't know, Melanie," she said, but she smiled a knowing sort of smile. "Maybe she's just having a little dalliance, a flirtation, you know, something to keep her occupied."

"Well, I shouldn't say anything, since she's your mom and all, but so what if she is, you know, having a bit of a thing?" Eliza said. "I mean, your dad took off, right? A girl's gotta do what a girl's gotta do."

Melanie sighed. "I don't know. I think Mom's been out of it too long. She doesn't know what she's doing. You should have seen her at Trina's. She was acting all into this loser guy. She was definitely totally flirting with him. Mom is too, I don't know, desperate or something." Jan and Eliza waited for her to go on, but Melanie could feel Erika bristle from across the table. She looked up from her iPad, with her stupid twisted-up-looking mouth, and her bugging-out eyes. Erika could never stand it when Melanie talked about their mother like she was an actual person. Erika was like a three-year-old in that way, unable to face that their mother was now single and maybe insecure about dating at her age.

Erika suddenly slammed the iPad case shut, and everyone turned. "Well, at least she's not a little . . ." And she paused, confused, unable to complete the sentence.

"A what?" Melanie hissed, glowering, leaning over the table. "Just say it, a little what?"

Erika shut her mouth tightly and stared back at Melanie. Her hands trembled a little on the tabletop, and Melanie could hear her tapping her bony feet against the hardwood floor. Melanie had pushed her too far. She had her cornered.

"A little slut!" Erika spat the words out and stood stunned at her own pronouncement.

———

Melanie grasped her wineglass, the thin stem fragile in her tense grip. It was everything she knew from the beginning. Erika hadn't told on her to Ms. Jensen out of concern for her. She didn't think she'd been a rape victim. It had all been her stupid babyish need to rat her out for anything she did. Erika was a spy. Erika was a loser tattletale baby who needed to keep everyone around her as innocent and as stupid as herself. She didn't care about Melanie, only about herself. Erika just couldn't stand not knowing, not understanding. She hadn't cared about what happened, so long as she could play the good girl and point at her as the bad one. The bad seed. The spoiled brat.

She hadn't meant to throw the whole glass, just the wine.

It had been one of those big round glasses that break so easily.

21

Erika liked the dry, antiseptic smell of hospitals. She even liked the triage process; it was sensible, scientific, if not altogether efficient. Unfortunately, Jan had been determined to take her to the new "concierge" emergency facility on Chambers Street, which had an atmosphere more like an airport lounge than a hospital emergency room. Erika had felt strangely out of place sitting in an upholstered arm-chair, cupping her bleeding face, while Jan filled out forms. It seemed like an eternity before the nurse ushered her out of the carpeted foyer and into the mostly empty, tiled triage room. There, she was told to sit with her head back while another nurse began to clean the wound and stop the flow of blood that had been trickling down the side of Erika's face, since the moment the sliver of glass had lodged into the side of her nose. At some point, she heard Jan's voice and felt her sister's hand on her shoulder. "Mom will be here soon. She's on her way downtown. I just spoke to her."

"Okay," Erika said. "Is she upset?"

"Of course she is!"

"What did you tell her?"

"Just that you and Melanie had a fight. I don't know exactly what was going on with you guys. Melanie was talking about Mom and then you were going after Mel. Was that about what happened at that party? She shouldn't have thrown the glass, Erika, but she feels terrible now. I'm sure she didn't mean it. I'm sure you didn't mean it either." Jan shook her head. "I guess I really should have talked to you guys before we came down. Seems like a lot of shit happened between you. I thought Eliza and I could talk to Melanie, but I guess we were bad influences on the drinking front."

When Jan spoke in her somber, reasonable voice, Erika deeply regretted calling Melanie that terrible name. She meant to be like Jan, understanding and even-tempered. Someone who understood without being told how other people felt. At the dinner table, that word had just flown into Erika's consciousness and lodged itself there, almost before she was aware of even being angry at Melanie. But why would Melanie talk about Mom like that? Or get into the sort of trouble she had with Gerald? What was wrong with her sister? Why did they see everything so differently? "I didn't mean it literally, I guess. But I had to say something when she started talking about Mom. She hates me anyway. She really does."

Jan stroked Erika's forehead, brushing her hair back, the way their mother would under the circumstances. It felt good to be taken care of, to be understood.

"Melanie has her way and you have yours, Erika. I think Melanie is really angry at Dad for ditching us the way he did, going off to Hong Kong right away, not letting anyone even get used to the separation. She's kind of out of control. She and Dad didn't exactly have the best relationship when he was home. I know you were trying to help her, but sometimes people have to get through things their own way. I know I let you down by not talking to Mel after you told me about that party. But I didn't want to do more harm than good, you know?"

"I know," Erika said. "You know, Dad emails us both every couple of days. It's not like he's abandoned us."

"I know he does. He's there for all of us, even though he's away. And I promise not to ignore anything from now on. I'll be there for you, too, okay? Even though I'm at school."

"Okay," Erika agreed. The first nurse came back to where Jan and Erika sat, and she ushered them into a small side room. The room contained a full-sized hospital bed, and a small fern by the bedside. It looked like a room intended for an extensive procedure, and not just a few stitches. "Jan, stay with me?"

"Of course, I'm right here."

The door opened and the doctor walked in, seemingly surprised to find them there. "Hey, girls," he said, and sat down on the stool beside the cot. "I'm Dr. Anderson. Dennis Anderson." He shook hands with Jan, and then leaned over into Erika's field of view. "You must be Erika," he said. He had curly brown hair, and small hazel eyes. Erika could see by the shape of his smile that he was trying to make her relax while he began his examination. His smile was hard at the edges, rectangular, and not soft and sloping like the smile of a truly friendly person. She trusted him immediately.

"So, your sister tells me your nose had some sort of encounter with a shard of glass."

"Yes."

"And she removed the glass from about here, and that's when this bleeding started? In other words, your nose wasn't bleeding first, right, all the blood is from the cut?"

"Yes. I'm not sure the whole glass even hit me. It's crazy, but I think it may have bounced into me. Hit a certain angle and then bounced up, I guess."

"Yes, it's crazy-sounding, but not impossible," the doctor said. "But it did result in a nice slash down the right side of your nose. Now, I am attending here right now, but I'm a plastic surgeon, so I think we'll wait a few minutes for your mom to arrive, so we can get her approval for the plastic surgery. Really, it simply means I'll stitch the cut on the inside of the skin to minimize any scarring. I know you must be concerned about a scar, honey, but I'll fix it so there'll just be the tiniest line—like a hair, down the side of your nose here." He traced the length of the cut with his forefinger.

"About how many stitches will you need to put in?" Erika asked.

She could feel the doctor's hesitation. "We'll see when we

get there. You know, the smaller the stitch the better. Could be fifteen, could be more. You have about a one-and-a-quarter-inch cut." He paused a moment, then leaned forward, his voice dropping slightly. "You know, honey, I'm required, in cases like these, to ask you girls to give a separate account of what happened. We have Jan's story already, but Erika, you need to give me your account of it, too. Then your mother will be given the statement. But since Jan is eighteen, she's considered the adult witness of the incident."

"I'm tired," Erika said, her voice breaking. "I'm sure Jan told you the whole story. She was right there." Erika had already determined not to say anything more to anyone ever about Melanie, least of all doctors. She could picture Melanie right now, sitting at their table with that pale, meat-loving Eliza from Montana. Melanie might blame herself now, or she might blame Erika for what happened. It didn't matter. She had tried to achieve an understanding with Mel through talking, even though words were difficult for her. Now she was going to try something new. Maybe there was something in the silence between them, in the physical space that they shared—maybe they could know each other and trust each other that way, like part of the herd, people who were physically but not emotionally close. Maybe she could learn to live with Melanie if she worked within that silence.

"Okay," the doctor said. "We'll assume that you girls were a little worked up, one of you knocked into the glass, and this was a sort of freak occurrence."

"Physics isn't really freakish," Erika said, "just sometimes hard to predict."

"Okay, then," the doctor said with a laugh, "there was an unpredicted outcome."

"That's the truth," Erika said, for the outcome was unpredicted, at least on her side. That Melanie wanted to hurt her had been evident for weeks. But she hadn't meant to say the words that brought Melanie to that moment of violence. She hadn't ever even thought that word before, and then it landed so improbably on her tongue. It was almost always words that betrayed people, she thought, not physics.

———

At first, it was Melanie who was pointing a toy gun at her, and then it was a man. He was Russian, but Erika did not know how she knew that. The gun was real then, but still looked like a toy. When the man pulled the trigger, the gun made a short popping noise, and she thought how small that sound was, considering she'd been shot at such close range.

She put her hand to her throat and began to call out. She was calling for her mother, but since she'd been shot in the larynx, she could only emit a strangled sob. Erika woke herself in that struggle to scream, choking on her own voice. It took a moment for her to realize the Russian man was a mere dream image, that her sister had not pointed a toy gun at her, that she was in no present danger. Her heart beat rapidly, though, so rapidly that she feared she had given herself a heart attack. Her face throbbed, especially the right side of her nose. It had been twenty-four hours since the doctor had stitched her up, and he had warned her that there could be some pain, especially at night, when lying still without ice allowed the swelling to build pressure beneath her stitches.

She needed an analgesic to reduce the swelling, but first there was the problem of her heart. She had to slow herself down. She placed her hand on her chest. She visualized the blood coursing through her arteries, into veins, and, finally, delicate capillaries. She got up and went into the bathroom and took a Motrin. Still, her breathing remained rapid. She thought then that she would just take a peek into her mother's bedroom. When she was a little girl she would sometimes sneak into her parents' room at night. She liked to see her mother's hair laid out on the pillow. She liked to hear her parents breathe.

She opened the door and there lay her mother alone. She was less beautiful in sleep than in the daytime, her mouth open, her teeth wet with saliva. Erika could feel, in the too-warm room, her heart begin to slow to a normal rate. She could count the beats now. She felt so much better with her heart rate slowing that she decided to sit on the pillows her mother had strewn on the floor next to the bed. She pulled some covers over herself from the section of the bedspread that lay draped onto the floor—her mother always kicked her covers off. She put her head down on the pillow and realized Maxwell was down there too, and she petted him until he curled up beside her. It was all just a bad dream, brought on by the pain in her face and a fear she had that lingered with her still, a fear that no matter what she did, Melanie would hate her for the rest of her life.

But for now, she needed rest. There was nothing more she could do to make things right with Melanie. There was no forgiveness in her own fast-beating heart—there was only room now for fear, and its opposite—rest, security—and she'd found that there, on the floor, with her little dog, beside her lonesome, sleeping mother.

22

Melanie didn't know where she was going. All she knew was that stupid Thanksgiving dinner was finally over and she needed to *escape*. She wasn't usually an early riser, but she'd woken at seven and immediately got out of bed. Jan and Eliza were asleep on the floor of the living room. The apartment was quiet. Thank God, Mom hadn't gotten up early. Melanie had dreaded seeing her hovering over her newspaper, drinking coffee, her petite shape shabby in yoga pants and a ratty sweater, a reminder of how Melanie had failed her. She could imagine her look, the big sad eyes, a look in them of almost childish disappointment. Oh, her mom had been fine throughout the holiday dinner—everyone had been—but she knew she'd only been given a reprieve so that the holiday wouldn't be completely ruined. Mom had already hinted at some "additional therapy" with Pat Landau, so Melanie could "work through her anger." But that was just because her mother didn't know what to do with her, didn't want to even have to *think* about her. She'd rather *pay* someone to deal with her than to actually act like a parent.

No, she was still the one nobody could look at—the violent one, the one who'd hurt someone, the one who'd left a scar.

Nobody seemed to know or care that Erika had ruined her life with her big mouth, with her pretending to be oh so worried about her.

Fuck them all.

———

Melanie pulled on her leather jacket. It had been a birthday present in the spring from both her parents, though she was sure her father had just gone along with the whole thing. It was black, a supple leather that was silky to the touch. She knew a jacket shouldn't matter to a person, shouldn't impart to one's own skin a certain thrill, but this jacket did. It felt so substantial, like a shield, or a cloak in one of those ridiculous movies where everyone has some magic power.

The doorman on duty was a substitute guy, probably because it was the day after Thanksgiving and they couldn't get anyone else to work. It was a relief not to have to make small talk with some member of the staff, someone who would want to know where she could possibly be going so early in the morning.

She didn't actually have any clue where she was headed. The air was brisk, colder than she'd thought, and she could feel the chill of the sidewalk through the soles of her Converse. She turned north. There were options to the north: SoHo, the West

Village, Chelsea. She could walk all the way to Washington Heights if she wanted, where her family had once lived many years ago, when she was only a baby. Only Jan remembered the Heights, and the mangoes they'd buy on the street, artfully cut into the shape of a flower.

So much had already happened by the time she was born. So much had already been decided. Her sisters had their places in the family all carved out. Jan was already the perfect daughter—the one who'd never stepped her toe out of line. What had her parents already known about Erika at one or two? That she was beautiful, no doubt. Maybe they already knew about her brain, too. That she was gifted, but that there was something different about her. Mom sometimes told stories about how long Erika could stare out the window, how at only eight months she had seemed to say "robin"—not *bird*, but the name of a particular bird. How Mom had insisted even when the pediatrician shook his head.

Mom and Dad were the sort of people who loved oddities like Erika, and do-gooders like Jan. But she was neither of those things. She didn't know what she was, really, but it was something, she thought, that was ordinary, but strong. That was what she felt inside herself, an enormous strength, an extra reserve that held her upright even in times like this, when she was so despised by those closest to her, she should have crumpled. It was a strength that took her to both good and bad places, to the room with the bear rug, and now out on her own in the November chill. It was a strength of passion, and not necessarily intellect, like her sisters. Maybe it could ruin her and save her at the same time.

She could feel the strength in her legs as they carried her up West Broadway into SoHo. The streets were deserted, which gave even the upscale restaurants an unfinished appearance, as though New York—Manhattan—were really only an illusion, and that without its hordes of tourists and cabs, its dishwashers and busboys, its shoppers and storekeepers, the entire city was waiting blankly, uncomprehendingly, like a girl at a dance with no one to talk to.

Melanie walked past the low, redbrick building on Thompson Street that her middle school had annexed as a gym. She recalled how back then she used to hang out more with Gerald even than Jess. How when the other girls were all dramatic over boys, and talking about who'd kissed who and who'd gone to what party, she'd always had Gerald. He wasn't part of the crowd that got invited to Lani Elliot's country house, where it was rumored several boys had gotten blow jobs from a girl who had opted, wisely, to begin high school someplace uptown. Melanie had never liked Lani, even back in grade school. Lani always had followers more than friends, and Melanie found herself to be incapable of being a follower. It was that strength in her, that elasticity, that made her defiant; it was also that part of her that could reach for a glass, and let it fly.

In her mind it had been self-defense. Erika had no right to call her foul names, to insinuate to Jan and in front of Eliza that there was something wrong with her, that she'd done something so wrong it had stained her permanently. Shit happened. That was something everybody said.

Melanie walked along Broadway through the Village. She passed the Mexican place with the tawdry door front in the shape of a sombrero. She passed through the NYU area, the cold, institutional buildings outsized against the Village town-houses, and she thought briefly of Jan and Adam. Hadn't Jan said something about Adam maybe going here, about his having some sort of breakdown at Harvard? She pictured Adam and his tall, hunched frame and imagined seeing him there on the corner of Eighth Street and Broadway. In her mind, she conjured him in place of the strange guy at the coffee cart, how Adam could be standing there drinking a cup of tea, and she could buy one too, and they could talk about all the bullshit people said about them, how people really knew nothing about other people, and how they should keep their big, fat, stupid mouths shut, and how hardly anyone knew how to do that these days. Everyone could say anything about you, as long as they seemed to be expressing *concern*.

Adam would understand, but he was not there, only the coffee cart guy, so Melanie ordered a tea, and the man smiled. He looked Indian or Pakistani, and his front tooth was broken off in a jagged line. Melanie wondered what had happened to it—had he fallen as a child, running from some horrible incident no American could picture, some stampede of people, some panicked crowd escaping a sudden blast in the heat of a marketplace? But what if it were something simple, like a rock thrown by a schoolyard bully, or someone close to him, a friend or a brother? Maybe another, bigger boy had dropped him on his face for calling him a name, or someone else thought they knew something about this man, something secret he had done, and the blow was the price he paid.

Melanie could ask the man and he could answer, but she would never do that. Pain and injury were private, she knew that. If someone told you the story of a scar, a part of them was lying. They would omit the moment of shock and fear, the crying, the beating of their heart, the desperate look around for someone to make it better.

There wasn't anyone there. When you woke in a strange room, what had happened, happened to you alone.

Why did they think they knew?

———

There were too many words for things that should be without them. Melanie turned on Fourteenth Street, for its wide, still-empty sidewalks, and walked west, though she hated to abandon her northerly march. Broadway was beginning to come to life, and she needed to be somewhere else, somewhere less congested, closer to the river. She'd gone past Jess's neighborhood, where she'd half thought she'd stop to text her friend, to have breakfast, do something normal people did. She hadn't thought of herself as running away, as missing from anyone's life, but she couldn't stop walking, couldn't lessen that strange, elastic strength that had overtaken her legs.

Erika had told Ms. Jensen and her mother that she, Melanie, had been raped by her friend Gerald at James Jamison's party. She had told them about finding her, half undressed on the white bear rug.

She remembered so little about that party, but she remembered that bear's open mouth. What had it been doing, she thought, when it was killed?

When Erika said the word *rape* it must have ricocheted around the room; it was a boomerang, or a bat.

Melanie could feel the word's dark presence on her.

———

It was clear to her now where she was going. She was going to Eighteenth and Sixth, past the animal hospital, and the store that sold fancy hats, past the Greek place on the corner that was gay only at night. She'd turn the corner on Eighteenth to the beautiful new building made entirely of glass, and she'd take out her phone and find the text that Gerald had sent that said only "This is my fifteenth text" because he sent one every day for two weeks, since she'd refused to speak to him at school, but then he'd stopped after the perp walk had turned him into a pariah. But now she hit reply and typed, "I'm outside your building."

She had the strength to do that, though her knees trembled slightly.

She ignored the five messages from home.

It was nine o'clock now, and they had discovered that she was missing.

Gerald answered the door in his socks and sweatpants. His hair was uncombed, as if he'd gotten Melanie's text in his sleep. He blinked rapidly as he opened the door to the apartment.

"My mom and brother went downtown to my grandmother's. I'm supposed to meet them there later." Gerald held up a note written in green marker. "My grandmother likes for us all to go to her place in the Hamptons for Thanksgiving, but my mom refused this year—so now we all have to go to their place in the Village for brunch. Like anyone wants brunch."

Melanie glanced out the window of the apartment to the terrace, which was just beyond the foyer. It was large enough to hold a Ping-Pong table, a table to eat at, and innumerable lounge chairs, and it had a view of the river. Melanie and Gerald used to have Ping-Pong tournaments when they were younger, and Gerald would get mad if he lost and deliberately hit the ball over the railing of the terrace. One time, the Ping-Pong ball had hit a homeless guy who was rooting through piles of garbage on the sidewalk below, and the guy had looked down at the Ping-Pong ball, and then up at the sky, shaking his fist, as though he'd been the target of some particularly petty god. Melanie had laughed so hard that day she'd cried.

Melanie sat on one of the stainless steel barstools like she had a hundred times before. Gerald sat beside her and half spun around. He looked at Melanie. She could tell he was trying to look relaxed, sitting on his kitchen stool, swinging his feet, but she could see that he was gritting his teeth. His eyes had a wild look that reminded her somehow of horses, and how she feared them for the way they unpredictably jerked their heavy-looking heads. Gerald's eyes were very blue, something she had never noticed about him before. She'd always thought of Gerald as sort of colorless, shaggy almost-blond hair, blue eyes almost gray but not quite. She had almost liked him for real once, back in eighth grade, and they'd even held hands at the movies, but he had bored her, always talking about his basketball games, and how they got too much homework, and they had gone back to being just friends.

"So, what?" he asked. "Do you hate me like everyone else?"

She paused, but did not answer him. "I thought I should tell you what I remember," she said. She hadn't thought about what it was she wanted to say, or even what she remembered of that night.

"Okay," he said. He stopped swinging his feet, and sat very still.

"I remember I told you to stop." This was both true and not true. It was something she surmised she must have done. "I told you no," she said louder.

"But you were kissing me." Gerald sounded whiny. "You pulled me in there, into that room." His voice broke, and he raked his hand through his hair, so that instead of smoothing it, he'd made it stand straight up.

"There was this boy who laughed at me. I remember want-ing to get away." This part Melanie was sure of. But she also vaguely recalled grabbing Gerald, wanting this other boy to see.

"You didn't say anything, and we kept doing more stuff, and you seemed into it, and . . . I thought you wanted it, too."

"Why?" she asked. It seemed to her he must have wanted to prove something, like she couldn't toy with him, or she somehow owed him that moment, and nothing less, as if it were the fact of their friendship that permitted him to have her against her will. It made her angry all over again, how he had taken from her something she couldn't take back. It wasn't fair. She was stronger than him, but she was still a girl.

"I'm trying to explain to you. I was wasted too, and we were messing around, and then . . ." He stopped, confused.

"Fuck you," Melanie spat. But to her horror, the strength that had gotten her there suddenly left her and she began to cry. "I know we were fooling around, I just don't know why you . . . you must have known I was too drunk. . . ."

"Fuck me?" Gerald got up from his chair and walked around the kitchen, his gray socks flopping off the ends of his toes. "Don't you understand?" He was both yelling and crying now, tears streaming down his face. "Don't you see how *you're* always using *me*?" His teeth were clenched and he let out a quiet moan. She noticed he looked slightly bruised under one eye, as though someone had hit him, but some time ago, and she wondered when. A silence settled between them.

"So basically you took your chance," Melanie said quietly.

Gerald kicked the legs of one of the kitchen stools and crossed his arms in front of him. "I was so fucking in love with you, okay? Always. For fucking ever. I made myself believe it was finally happening. That you didn't see me as a waste of time. But I'm really just a waste of Melanie Russell's breath!"

"I'm so fucking sorry for you," Melanie said. "But you are a waste of my time. You're pathetic." She spat the words at him, then backed out the door. She turned and walked toward the elevator with the door open behind her. She thought she could hear Gerald banging his fist against something, the wall or counter. Let him hit something, she thought. Let him have a hissy fit and break every glass, every dish. She pushed the elevator button and let out a choked sob. Then she felt strangely light.

It was over. The whole ordeal was over. She didn't have to think about that tiny twinge of guilt she'd had when Gerald said she'd thought he was a waste of time. That was the sort of thing she'd say to Jess about Gerald. But it wasn't something she thought Gerald ever knew. Maybe it was true that she used him in a way, that she liked having him like her, and hanging around her all the time. But now he had lost any right to complain. He didn't have the right to even look at her. She could go home, and eat a turkey sandwich, and do her English homework. She might even apologize to clueless Erika. It wasn't really her fault she couldn't understand anything about life.

━━━━━

At first, Jan didn't respond to the text from Adam. It was Friday evening, and she finally had a moment to herself. Eliza had volunteered to take Maxwell for a walk, and Melanie, Erika, and Mom all had work to do. Jan had a response paper to write for poetry, and reading for Early Romantics, but nothing too strenuous, and she and Eliza had the long train ride back to Providence to finish up any work she had left by Sunday.

She treated herself to a hot bubble bath, and a semi-nap, headphones on, eyes closed, and nothing to demand her attention but the soothing voice of Elena's Love, a band Jan heard about from Adam months before, but had never actually listened to. Then, as if conjured by the wispy voice of Elena Argent, Jan's phone buzzed after only a few minutes of peaceful wafting in and out of consciousness. It was Adam. In a cryptic text, he seemed to be suggesting a meeting: "Seems strange not to be in touch when I know you must be home," he wrote. Jan sighed.

Was it worth seeing him, if that was all he had to say? It was like their relationship was a habit that he found odd, although not especially painful, to do without. But there was something else about that text. There was the slightest hint in it of the old Adam.

———

Early Saturday morning Jan left Eliza a note. She didn't mention the plan beforehand, so she wouldn't feel the need to explain, or be subject to Eliza's possible judgment—that she needed Adam in order to have male attention, that she couldn't feel fully engaged in life without male approval, or some other theoretical nonsense, although Eliza had been relatively low-key since the fight between Melanie and Erika. Jan had filled Eliza in on what she knew about Melanie and the party, and Eliza had been surprisingly quiet. "Every girl has her own way of healing," Eliza had said.

Jan met Adam in the Village, at a diner near Rose Dyer. It was a place they'd been to only once or twice in the whole time they'd gone out, though it was just south of the Houston Street subway. Adam looked much the same as he had last month. Of course, Jan told herself. How much, after all, could he have changed? She felt oddly happy that she didn't feel attracted to Adam anymore. He looked pasty. She had, she discovered, developed a thing for dark-haired guys.

He stood waiting for her outside in the damp, cold air. "Thanks for coming," he began. "I wouldn't blame you if you never wanted to see me again." Jan shrugged and followed him into the diner. The booths were all taken, but Adam agreed when the waitress offered them seats at the counter. It wouldn't be a private conversation after all, but Jan surprised herself by feeling relief rather than rejection; she didn't require a long, deep conversation. She didn't want to stare into Adam's eyes. She took her seat and feigned interest in the generic diner menu. "So how was Thanksgiving? Did your dad come?" he asked.

Jan shook her head. "He comes back in a few weeks, though, for Christmas. I can't begin to describe Thanksgiving. Let's just say it wasn't boring." Jan couldn't see attempting to recount Eliza's presence, the fight between her sisters, Melanie's fit, the allegations about Gerald. It was all too personal now, although scarcely more than a month ago Adam might have been there himself to witness the entire scene.

"Well," he started again. "I wanted to say I'm sorry. For how things went. I mean a lot of what I said to you in Providence was true. It was how I felt. But I didn't want you to think nothing was real about the past. I didn't really mean any of that stuff about when we were together in high school." He drenched his pancakes in butter and syrup, leaned over his plate, and hungrily took a bite. He barely made eye contact with her. Jan nodded and eyed her suspiciously yellow scrambled eggs. She should eat something, she knew, but she felt too full from days of doing nothing but eating. Listening to Adam wasn't doing much for her appetite.

Adam wasn't saying the relationship was important or real now, she noted, only that it had been something real to him in high school. But high school hardly mattered. If there was one thing the first months of college had taught her, it was that no one cared anymore who you were back in high school. She wondered why she had come. Adam, with his long, awkward torso, his pale skin, his perpetually uncertain expression, was not what she was looking for. She knew that absolutely. Maybe Eliza, with her short attention span, would forget all about her hookup with Roberto, and he'd be free game. That was only a dream, though, a crush to pass the time, but it was something, something to add excitement to her life.

She didn't need to be stuck in Adam's unhappy world. As he explained what he had been doing the last four weeks, Jan felt fidgety. She moved her eggs around and took a sip of lukewarm coffee from the too-thick diner mug. Her life at Brown wasn't half bad. It was starting, even, to feel a little exciting.

"I'm tutoring at this school near my parents' place. In the nineties on West End. Eighth grade math. It's amazing," he was saying, still shoveling in large bites of syrup-sodden pancake. "I've got this one student, John. He's truly an enigma." Adam paused, eyes half shut in contemplation, a dripping forkful of pancake dangling midbite. "He seems bright. He can tell you anything you want to know about motorcycles. He draws them all over his notebook in perfect detail. Everything he draws is a Harley and he knows the exact models. I asked if his dad or anyone in his family had a bike, and he said no. But when he was a little kid some guy in his building had one and he parked it below the kid's window in some back alley. That's how the kid got into bikes. He'd sit there in his bedroom for hours, and look at this guy's bike, like it was the most beautiful thing in the world."

Jan realized Adam was strangely invested in this boy; his story had somehow become his own. "John told me he remembered this day the guy got on the bike, and it wouldn't start, and he started banging on the handlebars, and then he got off it, and started kicking it, and John started crying and yelling at the guy and his mom had to come into his room and make him stop. I asked him how old he was when this happened and the kid said he was maybe four years old. Amazing, right? He remembers this whole story, every detail of it. But the kid knows absolutely nothing about math. Not even multiplication."

Jan smiled vaguely. She couldn't tell whether Adam found the boy's story sad or simply fascinating. "I guess he didn't go to very good schools, and now it's up to you to get him caught up. That's really meaningful," she said. She wanted Adam to think she admired him for doing what he was doing, or at least to not think she thought he was a loser for dropping out of college.

Adam shook his head. "This kid is like the Hercules of not learning. I'm no match for him. But anyway, it's something to do. I'm applying to Columbia and NYU for next year. I'm thinking about living at home for a semester, then maybe easing back into school. My parents are okay with it. They seem to think I had some traumatic experience I'm not talking about. Like a bad trip."

"Well, there was that," Jan said. "I mean, we did those 'shrooms."

Adam shook his head. "No, that was clarifying to me. It was that night I knew I was doing the right thing. I still think you and I are in very different places." He had finished his pancakes, but was still swirling his fork in the crumbs that were left sticking in the golden syrup. Jan watched him. Where had he gone? He wasn't the same boy she'd dated in high school. Adam had been serious then, but never like this, never telling random stories and talking himself down. He was depressed—it was like the articles she sometimes read in the *Times* about people who became detached, people who felt miles away from other people. That was how Adam talked, like she was emotionally distant from him, more distant than this boy, John, with his sad obsession. It was both annoying and flattering the way Adam seemed to see her, like she lived on planet normal, and he lived somewhere else, a place that was painful and static, a kind of nowhere. The way he talked about John, it was almost like he was in competition with him and the kid was the expert, the one who really knew how to lose at life.

A part of Jan still wanted to be exotic, like Eliza and the other girls who dressed up for the slut walk night, or like Mr. Stainless and his dreadlocked girlfriend, someone known all around campus for her hipness or her brilliance. But she also knew she was changing. She felt on the edge of something, only she didn't know quite what. If it was a new romance, that would be awesome, but it was okay if she was on the romantic sidelines for a while too. It was fun to scope guys out, live out imagined entanglements.

Jan insisted on paying for breakfast, although she knew this might be a cruel reminder to Adam of his past money obsession. She didn't care, though. If she were the normal person in the relationship, why not embrace that? Why not make it the thing she had to offer?

———

Erika put her hand to her face. Her nose was still tender to the touch, but the stitches were small, like the doctor had promised; they formed a thin, dark line, almost perfectly straight and hardly wider than a hair's width.

"If you stop messing with that shit, no one will even notice it," Morris said. Erika and Morris were studying European history in Morris's room. They were supposed to have a test the Tuesday they got back from Thanksgiving break, and Morris needed the notes. Sometimes, Morris and other people fell asleep during history. Cynthia Barrow was the most boring teacher at RD. Unlike the other teachers, she tended to lecture almost every class. It was like she was blind to the fact that half the class was slumped in their seats becoming catatonic. Erika liked Cynthia, though. She was like a teacher in a movie about teachers, the way she stood in the front of the room and talked, and wrote on the Smart Board. She even dressed like a movie teacher, in tight-fitting skirts with conservative blouses, hair pulled back in a ponytail, glasses perched on the end of her nose, as though there only as proof that without them she would be prettier. Erika enjoyed being in Cynthia's class and playing the made-for-the-movies part of the excellent student, the girl who almost always already knew whatever the teacher was talking about.

"These aren't even notes," Morris said, shaking his head at Erika's notebook pages. "This is a freaking exact transcript. You should take notes for the United Nations, or the Supreme freaking Court or some shit." He took a bite from a piece of the pecan pie he had on his desk and shook his head in self-disgust. "If I eat any more of this pie, I'm going to be sporting a Big Daddy Foss-style belly. That is no look for a young, single man in his physical prime." Erika laughed and took a big bite from her own plate. She was eating both apple and pumpkin pie. "Your dad practically made me take half of each pie," Erika said. "He told me I'd be doing him a service. He said he ordered like six of them."

"Damn right," Morris said. "The dude is getting to be an embarrassment. I mean, there is a gym right here in the building, and he employs this guy, Fred, practically full-time to keep him on track, and he's still the inflatable man."

Erika contemplated her plate. The pie was good, but she figured if it made her overweight, it wouldn't be that hard to give it up. She was lucky she never gained weight. She could hardly ever recall feeling like she was overly full, even after a large meal. It was yet another way she didn't relate to a lot of other girls. When Binky expressed dismay about her figure, or Jan or Melanie did, Erika always kept silent. It reminded Erika of the silence that had fallen over the Russell apartment since Friday morning, when Melanie and Jan suddenly reappeared after both being absent without explanation.

Mom didn't question Melanie at all. But Melanie had seemed okay. She'd gone to her room and played her music loud. Erika liked having Jan and even Eliza around the house, but it was messy and disorganized with them there, with their shoes and coats always strewn around the living room. She vaguely looked forward to a return to her regular routine, especially now that Mom and Melanie seemed to be working together on Melanie's problems. It was all out of Erika's hands. Although Melanie had made good on her threat to hurt her, even that was done now. She had hurt her, but it hadn't seemed exactly intentional. Erika unconsciously fingered the scar on the side of her nose. Again, Morris barked at her.

"Erika, stop touching that shit already! It's giving me the

willies! I hate blood and stitches and all that hospital crap."
Morris shut his textbook, stood up, and stretched. His pet birds
all sat in two large cages by the window, and Morris leaned into
the bigger cage and poked the male cockatiel, coaxing it onto
his finger until it perched there. He withdrew his arm from the
cage and stood still, showing Erika how tame the bird was, sitting on the end of Morris's finger, preening. It was tricolored,
with a patch of yellow near the leg joint, while the rest of the
body was blue, melding into the red feathered crown. The bird
tilted its head and eyed Erika with its wide, yellow eye.

Erika didn't mind the birds but worried the cockatiel might
perch on her head again, and maybe even peck at her stitches.
"What do you think I should say, Morris, when people ask me
what happened?" The bird had seemed to be eyeing the black
line of stitches. If the bird noticed the stitches, surely people
would as well.

"To mind their own fucking business," Morris said. "Except
that never works with anybody." He stroked the bird's back with
a single finger. "How about, my psycho-bitch sister tried to one-
eye me? Got in a knife fight at a bar? The turkey fought back?
Lots of options." Morris continued stroking the bird's back
while he spoke, seemingly lost in thought.

"Seriously, Morris. I don't want everyone to talk about it.
There's already been a lot of drama about Melanie and Gerald. I
probably shouldn't have even told you or Binky about the fight
with Melanie."

"You got nothing to worry about there," Morris said. "This

whole Gerald-Melanie drama is just sad. It'll be lucky if that Gerald kid doesn't off himself. Tell you what. I will personally beat the crap out of the next person at RD who says anything about you, your sister, fucking Gerald, James Jamison, or that goddamn Halloween party. That shit is over. That shit is done."

"You're going to beat people up, Morris?" Erika said, shaking her head. "But you're a pacifist. That's what you always say."

"Uh-huh, a lover not a fighter, true that. But I think it's time to shut this show down. You say Melanie is good, right? You have nothing more to worry about than this test Tuesday, and applying some scar-be-gone crap on that scrape. I'm the one around here with worries. This dude has some nasty little mites crawling up his little bird butt. Look at them here. Tiny little birdy ass bugs. Yuck." Morris made a disgusted face and held the bird at a further arm's length, averting his head. "I've got bird ass bugs in my pie. That is what I call an actual problem that requires immediate attention."

Erika laughed as Morris sprayed the cockatiel with birdbath spray. The bird spread his wings and puffed out his chest as though waiting for another dousing. He liked it and Morris kept spraying him so the bird shook his tail feathers, flapped, and made low, chuckling sounds. "That's right, Mr. Bird, you go ahead and sing in your shower. Flap your wings and sing, you bird-bug-infested fuck. Morris is going to clean you right up, or you're going out that motherfucking window."

Erika shook her head. Morris was not the best pet owner, but the bird didn't seem to mind. "You're not even getting any on his butt," Erika said. "You've got to turn him around. Here, let me do it." She took the spray bottle from Morris, and while Morris cooed to the bird, she sprayed his back and tail feathers until they dripped with spray. Morris was probably right, Erika figured. Neither she nor Melanie wanted anyone else to know what had happened between them, and so no one had to know. The bad things that had happened didn't have to live on and on in everybody's minds. If people and animals, insects and universes—even bird mites—all had a life span, couldn't experiences, memories, and feelings have life spans too? Couldn't feelings simply die?

23

The snow was not supposed to begin until after seven, but at five in the afternoon it had already begun to flurry, and by five-thirty the storm had hit full force. The forecast was for a wild night, with blizzard conditions and nonstop snow. Some schools had already canceled classes for the next day, but not RD, or at least not yet. Melanie had just finished track club. They met in one small section of the gym and then ran, idiotically, around the school building, up and down stairs, sprinting through empty hallways. There would be only two meets with other track clubs for the entire season. It wasn't like being on a varsity sport, but Melanie had blown off track tryouts the year before, and after having done nothing but paint scenery for the school play last spring, Melanie felt she should join something. It wasn't only because colleges liked to see that you were a joiner of some kind. But also, sad to say, Melanie had gotten bored. She felt a little out of shape. Suddenly, in the last six months, her body had thickened. She wasn't the girl she once was. It was especially bad when she was getting her period. Then, her jeans sometimes didn't fit at all.

Jess had flat feet and refused to do track club with her. Jess claimed that flat-footed people couldn't run no matter what kind of shoes you put on them. Running on her feet, Jess claimed, was like running on hands. But there were some older girls who did track club, and Erika's friend Binky, who was tolerable to run with, at least, had been there today.

Melanie changed into her Uggs in the locker room and brushed out her hair. She had worn a knit hat with a funny red pompom that she had found with Jess at a thrift store in Williamsburg. But she hadn't worn a warm coat, only a thick sweater, one that was too thick to fit under her parka. Her mother had said something about the snow this morning, but Melanie hadn't listened. The sweater had a thick turtleneck and a black band around the cuffs. She'd looked cute with only the pompom hat and her thick black leggings, like a girl from a fifties movie, where they go skiing in the alps and sit around rustic fireplaces. But now she'd have to face the brisk wind, and the snow that was becoming steadier by the minute. Outside, the wind lashed her face, and the snow stuck to her eyelashes. She hesitated a minute at the heavy red door of the gym, as though contemplating ducking back in, when a boy burst out of the boy's locker-room exit. It was Edward, and Melanie blushed at the sight of him.

"Hey, kid!" Edward loped toward her. He was zipped into a

large black parka, with the hood pulled up, so he looked like an Arctic explorer, with only his eyes unconcealed. She could tell, however, that beneath the coat's heavy collar, he was smiling his crooked smile at her, being irresistibly friendly.

"Well, you're ready for this," Melanie said, regaining her composure. The snow was already accumulating underfoot.

"Can't say the same for you," Edward said, smirking at Melanie's already soggy sweater. "Wait, maybe I can save your ass. I'd give you my excellent parka, but you don't deserve it. Anyway, I don't trust you to return a thing of such extreme value." Melanie giggled. She had seen Edward in passing in the hall, but since all the trouble with Gerald, she'd been too shy to say hello, and so she'd turned her head whenever she thought he might glance her way.

Edward fumbled around in his backpack, and then pulled out an enormous fleece-lined red and blue RD winter varsity track sweatshirt. "Put this on," Edward said.

"This is the most ridiculous thing ever," Melanie said, as Edward pulled the sweatshirt over Melanie's head. It went down to her knees, but she was instantly warmer.

"Come on," Edward said, "I'll walk you." He struck out in the direction of her subway stop on Houston, rather than his stop, which would have been up Sixth Avenue, by the movie theater, but Melanie didn't say anything about Edward going out of his way.

The wind had picked up and it was difficult to see or talk. Melanie walked with her head down, close to Edward, until they turned a corner toward the river and were blasted in the face by an arctic gust. Even Edward was blown backward. "Here, duck in!" Edward called. He pulled Melanie by the sleeve into a nearby store. It was a quiet place on a corner that was always something new. Now, it was a place that sold hot and cold tea in every imaginable flavor. It was empty in the shop, except for the shopgirl, who busied herself behind the counter arranging already neatly arranged paper cups. Edward and Melanie stood by the door staring out at the swirling snow.

"I guess it won't get any better," Edward said.

"No," Melanie agreed. "Not like we can wait it out. We'll be here all night."

"Okay," Edward said. "Next time it looks even minutely less windy, we'll make a run for it. We only have about another block or so." Snow melted off Melanie's hat and into her eyes. Her legs were already sore from running and she wanted to be home, to take a hot shower and change into dry clothes. Mom, she knew, had a late meeting in midtown. She'd said so this morning. Melanie didn't mind being home alone; even if Erika were there, that would be okay. Things had been quiet between the two of them. It seemed like Erika felt almost as bad about calling Melanie a slut as Melanie felt about throwing the glass. When it was just the two of them in the apartment in the evening, it made Melanie wonder what it might be like to be in her twenties and have a job and a roommate.

"Do you ever wonder where you'll be in, like, ten years?" she asked Edward, following her own internal train of thought.

"All the time," he said. "I know I won't be here, though."

"You mean here in the city, or here in this particular tea shop?"

Edward laughed. "The city," he said. "I'm not a city guy."

"Really?" Melanie said. "Then what kind of guy are you?" She realized what she said sounded flirty, but it popped out before she could think of something else.

Edward contemplated her, and knocked some snowflakes off her hat. "I don't know. I like it up in Massachusetts where we have our place. But maybe I'll travel a lot. Have a job doing some kind of computer stuff, you know, consulting."

For some reason, it always made Melanie sad when people talked about moving away from New York. She took it almost personally, as though her presence there in the city should make it attractive to anyone she knew. But she suppressed the feeling. It wasn't right to let some random thing Edward said hurt her feelings. "That's like my dad," Melanie said. "He writes. He's in Hong Kong now." When she mentioned her father, Melanie teared up without knowing why. "He's coming back for Christmas, at least to visit, I'm not sure. He says he's moving back soon. But he was always away anyway. I mean before my parents split up." She was rambling, not sure why she was saying any of this to Edward.

"When my dad died, the actual day he died," Edward said, "it was snowing like crazy, like this. Lots of people, his brothers, his aunts, wanted to come down and sit with him at the hospital, but they couldn't get here. It was weird. Like here he was dying, but all anyone could talk about was the weather. It was one of those storms just like this, where everyone goes rushing around like the end of the fucking world."

"I don't know why people do that," Melanie said. "It's New York City. Duh. There's how many grocery stores?"

Edward didn't say anything for a minute, but stared out the window. "I think it's our moment," he said. "Ready to make a run for it, little girl?"

"It looks awful," Melanie said. She was wet through to her skin, and though she knew she wasn't warming up in the tea shop in her wet clothes, she had trouble forcing herself back outside.

"Yup," Edward said. "But, as you said, we can't stay here all night."

"Right," Melanie said. "I'm bracing myself."

"All right," Edward said. "Tell you what. Since you remain miserably underdressed, and I'm practically ready for Everest, I'll lead the way. Hold on to me, and try not to wipe out, because we're going to make a serious run for it." Melanie laughed.

Edward gave Melanie his gloved hand and pushed open the heavy glass door. The snow immediately blew in their faces, but Edward pushed ahead. They ran down the block, Edward out in front, hooded, with the snow accumulating on his book bag, dragging Melanie behind. Melanie half shut her eyes and screamed, her feet slipping with every step.

They ran down the block slipping on the thin layer of snow, and when they went down the subway steps Melanie still clung to Edward's arm. In the station, she took off her hat, and shook the snow from it. Her wet hair clung to the side of her face, and she struggled to catch her breath. Edward shook the snow from his hood and sleeves. He had been kind and open with her, but now he became distracted, as though he didn't know how it was he'd ended up with her at the wrong subway station. Melanie started to take off the sweatshirt to return it to Edward, who needed to go uptown, while she was going downtown. "Oh no, you wear it. It's even clean. You'll freeze in only a sweater. If I were really heroic, I'd have gotten us a cab. But I'm a cheap bastard."

"You've been really nice, though," Melanie said. "Thanks."

"Modern chivalry demands these things," Edward said. "I don't think stupid little girls should be left to freeze to death just because they lack the sense to wear coats, like people with truly developed central cortexes." Melanie chuckled and looked away.

"I guess it was fairly stupid," Melanie said. "It seemed like a good idea in the morning. They said it would snow later tonight. I took a gamble."

"Well, anyway, there's something I wanted to say to you, and I never see you around anymore." Melanie's heart skipped a beat. She told herself she was being absurd. He thought of her as a child, Gerald's friend, and besides, he knew everything that had happened, just like everyone else at school. He was in love with Volleyball Ellen. He was there because, like everyone else, he pitied her.

"I wanted to tell you . . . ," he started, then stopped, and began again. "I wanted to say that one of the things I really hated about when my dad died is how everyone talked about it. Not people who knew him, but everyone else, like it was a big deal to them that he died, not because they cared about my dad, but because what happened to him made them think it could happen to them, too. They came to the funeral looking all shitty. But it wasn't about missing my dad, or him as a person. It was that death was all around, like some fucking monster. Like we were all in some freaky movie and my dad was the first to go, but some terrifying beast was coming back around for them. It made me want to puke." He paused for a moment, and looked around the nearly deserted subway station.

He took a deep breath. "There were other people who seemed less scared than shocked. That really got me pissed. It was like he wasn't a human being. Like he was different from all of them, weaker than them, because he got cancer. It really isn't shocking that people get sick and die. I mean it happens to fucking everybody at some point.

"Anyway, that's when people suck. When they say things without thinking. That's what I wanted to say. I think most people are"—he paused for a moment searching for the word—"selfish. They don't really think about how it is for you, when you're part of the story of something bad that happened. They just think about how they would never let something like that happen to them. Like people could be too good or too smart to die. Or, you know, get fucked up. Anyway, I didn't want you to think that was everyone. That no one saw what was happening at school."

An express train passed and shook the platform where they stood. Melanie wiped her eyes. She didn't want to cry, but the tears kept coming.

She shook her head, and forced herself to look straight at Edward. Of all the people at school who'd talked about her and Gerald, almost no one had said anything to her directly, or at least nothing she had wanted to hear. It was hard to listen to Edward's sympathy. Even though she thought about him, thought about him too much, she had never imagined he ever thought about her, thought about her as a person more or less like himself, someone who might suffer in the same way he had.

"At least now maybe people can find something else to talk about. They'll talk about the blizzard, and everyone will forget."

"Yeah," Edward said and shrugged. "Some crap."

"Well, thanks for the sweater. I mean sweatshirt. Fleecy thing," Melanie said.

"It's yours until you wash it," Edward said. "And then you've got to give it back. No stealing and shit."

"It's not really my size anyway," Melanie said. She hugged Edward, his wet parka pressing against her, and his cheek wet against her cold face. She kissed him on the cheek; he didn't kiss her back, but pulled on her wet pompom. Then he paused for a minute, seemed disoriented, and jogged up the steps and back outside to the uptown station.

Melanie smiled to herself and swiped through the turnstile. She looked forward to getting home, and curling up on her bed.

Her mother had texted her when the snow started that she might come home earlier than expected, but that she shouldn't worry, and the trains were all running fine. She hoped her mother had left something she liked for dinner, like chili. She wouldn't even mind if she made the vegetarian kind that Erika would eat, so long as there was plenty of hot sauce and sour cream.

The one train came quickly. The car was practically empty; so many people had gone home early in preparation for the storm. It was good to be inside and warm, if only for a few stops.

———

Upstairs in her building, Melanie used her key to let herself in, but strangely, the door was unlocked. It wasn't like Erika to leave the door open, even if she only went outside for a minute. Then Melanie noticed by the side of the door a snow-covered pair of man-sized Timberlands. Someone was over. At first, Melanie figured it must be Morris, but as she opened the door she heard a familiar gravelly voice.

It was her father, sitting across from Erika at the dining room table sipping a cup of tea. His hair was rumpled. He looked a good deal thinner than he had over the summer. His jeans and sweater were baggy on him. He turned toward Melanie as she shut the door, his smile bright at the sight of her.

"Dad?" Melanie called. He stood and opened his arms. There were no suitcases anywhere, no evidence of what he was doing there. Just Dad slightly unshaven, his glasses lopsided as usual.

"So come on!" he called. "Give us some love! Not every

day your old man pops in from halfway across the world!" He chuckled as she hugged him. He pulled off her snow-covered hat and tossed it toward the door, where it fell with a wet thud.

Erika shook her head and scolded. "Dad, you're making a mess and you don't even live here!"

"I know!" he said. "That's the beauty of it. I'll scram out of here before I get in any trouble."

"Oh, forget that," Melanie said laughing. "I've tried that, and in this family someone is always coming after you!"

"That's my girl," Dad said, keeping his arm around Melanie's sodden shoulder. "Keeping everybody on their toes." Melanie smiled uncertainly. She wasn't sure what Dad knew. She was relieved, at least, that he didn't seem angry at her.

"If you're not staying here, Dad, where are you staying—for how long?" Melanie asked. She had told herself she didn't miss her father. But now that she saw him, she felt herself choking up at the thought of him leaving.

"I'll be at Liam's until I find a place. Pretty great, right? I've got the first draft of the book done. No need to go back to Hong Kong for at least six months. I can make myself a big pain in both your asses, effective immediately."

"That's awesome, Dad," Melanie said facetiously, as she started to peel off Edward's snow-covered fleece.

"I think you need to deposit yourself in the shower," Dad said, nudging Melanie away from the dining room rug. Melanie nodded and started toward the bathroom.

Outside, the wind was blowing the snow down in sheets.

Melanie was thankful for the warmth of the apartment, for her father's presence. She was tired and hungry from running. She was tired of thinking about Gerald and Edward and kids at school. She was tired of her life being one big "situation." Dad was back in New York. This was a simple fact and it was good. It meant that life had changed, but that some things, at least, could change back, like the way some roads have wide spaces where cars can turn around.

"Dad, how about doing the heroic-dad thing and ordering us some Chinese food? I'm freezing and I want some hot-and-sour," Melanie called from down the hall.

"You can't ask Dad to do that," Erika called after her. "He's visiting. He doesn't live here, Mel!"

"I know that!" Melanie shouted. "But he's still my father! He can still buy the Chinese food!"

Dad laughed. "She's got a point there, Erika. She's the boss, after all. She's always going to be the boss!"

After a hot shower, Melanie changed quickly into dry clothes, and brushed out her knotted hair. Her father was home! The reality was gradually sinking in. He was there, ordering her dinner, waiting for her! She put on a pair of fleece-lined slippers and pinned her hair up in a bun. Outside, the snow fell heavier than ever. She could barely see the lights of even the closest buildings. Her view of the ice-covered river had been completely obliterated. The city would be shut down. Tomorrow would feel like a holiday. The snow was never beautiful for long in the city. It would soon turn brown and slushy and she would curse it when she walked to the subway. For one day, though, it would be pure. Her heart raced with a childish joy at the thought of a snow day, at the thought of her father's return. He was bound to be annoying. He always was. For now, though, Melanie felt light at the thought of having her father home. It was amusing to have him surprise them. It was like when they were little and took walks around the neighborhood. He would race ahead, act like he was running away, then duck behind the side of a building, jumping out at the last minute and enjoying their shocked delight.

Afterword

WHAT READERS SHOULD KNOW ABOUT RAPE, SEXUAL ASSAULT, STRANGER RAPE, NONSTRANGER RAPE, DATE RAPE, ACQUAINTANCE RAPE, AND SEX WITH A DRUNK OR OTHERWISE INCAPACITATED PERSON

ALL OF THE ABOVE ARE RAPE.

Although all of the above are rape in the legal sense, only stranger rapes are regularly reported and prosecuted; rates of prosecution for stranger rape are relatively high, at about eighty percent. Prosecutions for nonstranger rape between minors, when drinking is involved, occur only in the most egregious cases, usually highly publicized gang rapes. Rapes such as the one described in *The Word for Yes* are not reported by victims except in very rare cases. Because such rapes are not generally reported, the focus on such crimes has been on prevention.

Nonstranger rape prevention has generally focused on victim behavior. Prevention programs are not victim-blaming since the advice comes prior to, and with the intention of avoiding, assault. Girls are, rightly, warned not to drink heavily at parties, not to drink punch or other mixed drinks. Rape prevention experts are also critical of the "hookup culture" that seemingly gives would-be rapists both opportunity and cover for their crimes. Because "everyone is doing it," and the lines are "blurry," boys believe they can get away with rape.

In the story you have just read, the boy is portrayed as a "decent" person. He cares for his victim, and is her friend. He rationalizes that it is Melanie who uses him, and he who earnestly likes Melanie. This, however, does not give Gerald the right to behave as he does, which is criminal, even if he is also drunk.

Admittedly, if neither of the principal characters were drunk, there would have been no rape. In this sense, alcohol is a character in *The Word for Yes*. So is human desire. All of the characters, in some way or another, discuss or demonstrate a struggle to both satisfy and control desire, whether it is a desire to spend money (or not), eat certain foods, or have sex. Coping with desire is part of being human. Coping with desire when one is also drinking or using drugs complicates this issue. Alcohol and drugs both produce a self-sustaining desire for more of the substance, making a person tend not toward satisfaction, but toward greater incapacitation, along with a steady or increasing desire to consume more. This is what makes drugs and alcohol dangerous—the more you have, the more you want. At the same time, the more you consume, the less able you are to control your *other* desires—whether these are for sex or food or to run naked through the streets. Many young people (and older people) feel that they can control their human desires, even when drunk. This may be partially true, but it is never wholly true for anyone, and it is especially untrue of young people, whose developing brains are not as well-designed for self-control as older people's.

I believe if you are reading this novel, something like what happened to Melanie has already happened to you, or your best friend, or to someone else you know—perhaps your mother, or your aunt, or a favorite teacher. I can guarantee you that a woman you love and respect has been raped. I guarantee you that a man you respect and love has been in Gerald's situation. How he may have ultimately behaved is his secret.

Everyone has secrets. Rape is a secret a lot of people share.

There are many reasons girls and women do not report non-stranger rape, especially when alcohol is a factor. This is not an irrational response, since the process a girl needs to go through to press rape charges is very public, and if her memory is vague, this can be problematic. Also, as in Melanie's situation, friends and family will all be affected by the rape charges. The rape will become the victim's whole life.

If the criminal justice system is not a good option for many victims of nonstranger rape, what can be done after such a rape occurs? This is a tough question, and many, many feminists and legal experts disagree about how such rapes should be handled. One thing you need to remember is good self-care. Although a rapist should never "get away with it," the number-one person you need to show care and respect for is yourself. Here are some pieces of advice most experts agree upon:

You must get to a women's health clinic to receive tests for STDs and a pregnancy test. Ask your best friend, your mom, your aunt, your pediatrician, or your guidance counselor to help you do this. Find someone in your life you trust and who will not judge you. If you can't think of anyone, be your own best friend and take yourself to the clinic. The people who work at women's health clinics are your trained allies.

See a therapist who is trained in this area and who works with people your age. People who work with teens will know this area well. They will know all about what happens at parties, at prom, in basements. They will be there for you. If you don't know who to call in your area, contact the National Sexual Assault Hotline at 1-800-656-HOPE (4673). National hotlines will put you in touch with local specialists.

Do not attempt to confront your attacker in the way Melanie does. Remember, this is a novel. Melanie has weaknesses, and her main weakness is that she thinks she's a lot tougher than she really is! Although she feels relieved after confronting Gerald, many people would not. Also, in this case, Gerald really has feelings for Melanie, feelings of desire that have been frustrated and become anger. It's pretty complicated, so you do not want to confront your attacker alone. However, you will want to address this issue of confronting your attacker with your therapist.

Don't blame yourself. If you were drunk, blame yourself for being drunk, but not for getting raped. Don't blame yourself for being "a bad victim" and not going to the hospital or the police.

As a victim of nonstranger rape, all of your choices are tough. If there were clear "right" choices, everyone would make them.

Get involved. Rape prevention is meaningful work. Nonstranger rape is truly an epidemic. We live in a permissive society. Kids drink and "hook up." Lots of kids (and adults) don't have great boundaries. They flirt, kiss, and do other stuff. (By the way, it was like this before the internet, and before they called it hooking up.) But even hookup culture has its rules. People *do* know right from wrong. Even drunks know when they're being jerks.

Remember that *you* have rules for your own behavior and you have boundaries. Be honest and up-front about them. Remember things don't "happen" at parties, people *do things* at parties.

Be honest with yourself about your intentions before you go out drinking. Remember that self-care requires honesty. If you're going out to look for Mr. Adorable, he's probably not the guy who is downing ten beers. Girls and women are sometimes attracted to guys who appear strong, independent, and unattainable. If he seems unattainable, he probably is. If you hear him talk about other girls or women in a derogatory manner, listen up. If he isn't nice to his mom, pay attention to that too. You don't change people or control people by being smart, beautiful, and sexy. The most desirable women in the world get raped. Your good looks, charm, and personality will not protect you or win a guy over, if that guy is only looking for sex. Partying feels like magic, but that's just the substances talking to your animal brain. Magical things that happen between people happen when you're sober.

Guys need education (and healing too). Teaching boys and men to not even think about having intercourse with incapacitated girls and women will take time. Men who are drunk cannot use drunkenness as *either* an excuse for their actions *or* an opportunity to satisfy sexual desire. If you're talking to a guy who claims that being drunk *is* an excuse because guys get overwhelmed by desire and *can't* control the impulse, you need to confront this erroneous thinking. There are lots of things people do not do in public even when very drunk. Think about it. If other physical impulses can be controlled, sexual satisfaction can be controlled.

When you go to a party with friends, keep an eye on one another. Melanie's night goes awry when she wanders off to flirt with James Jamison. Her sister and her friends, who were supposed to keep an eye on one another, failed to do that.

Drugs and alcohol are a fact of youth culture, and American culture in general. But these substances are strong and mind-altering and affect different people differently. If you do choose to drink, think twice about playing drinking games, doing shots, or drinking "punch" or hard liquor in general. Alcohol is fast-acting and potent. If drugs and alcohol play a large part in your social life, and you feel your partying has put you in harm's way, think about how you can change this behavior. Changing behavior we feel guilt and shame about is hard. It is actually easier to continue to behave in the same guilt- and shame-inducing manner than it is to change your behavior, since changing your behavior and acknowledging the need to change means facing your guilt and shame head on. Remember that changing your behavior means renouncing your actions, not who you are, your friendships, or your entire past. Even if your past contains harm (as everyone's does), your past also contains a reservoir of experience, strength, and knowledge. There are numerous characters in this book, and they all have a point of view about rape and what it might mean for Melanie and Gerald. I do not believe any character in this book has it all right or all wrong. Certainly, no person in real life can tell anyone else how to feel about something that happened to them. Sometimes, when people are trying to help us, their help hurts. I gave my character Melanie what some people call strong boundaries. She is affected by what other people say and do, but she is not devastated by criticism or her public humiliation. As my own teenage daughter likes to say, embarrassment does not have to hurt. Melanie knows this intuitively, and it helps her move on. Other people, however, are sometimes very sensitive to the opinions of others, and may have more difficulty moving forward than Melanie does.

Another issue that is only touched on in this book is the role of social media in sexual assault. Social media as a forum for the sexual exploitation of girls and women is a relatively new phenomenon, and so adults tend to react with great alarm when gossip becomes "viral" and includes images. The idea that there is a public record of our most shameful, hurtful moments in life is, naturally, devastating. The upside is that this sort of thing, posting nude or drunk pictures, tagging girls as "hoes," has become so common that it is almost normative. Essentially, if everyone is a hoe, no one is a hoe.

We are all somewhat mysterious, even to ourselves, and that makes it hard to be a human being, and to really know ourselves and to really know others, but this deep sense of self is also what makes us resilient and helps us recover from shattering life events. Whoever you are, you are deep and dark and full of wonder. You cannot be fully exposed to anyone, even if you have been victimized. You are safe within yourself. At the end of *The Word for Yes*, Melanie's dad jokingly calls her "the boss." Melanie is bossy and mean sometimes. This is her biggest flaw. However, seeing herself as the boss of her own life, even when she makes multiple mistakes, is what gives her the power to heal herself and forgive herself for putting herself in harm's way.

JOIN THE

Epic Reads
COMMUNITY

THE ULTIMATE YA DESTINATION

◄ **DISCOVER** ►
your next favorite read

◄ **MEET** ►
new authors to love

◄ **WIN** ►
free books

◄ **SHARE** ►
infographics, playlists, quizzes, and more

◄ **WATCH** ►
the latest videos

◄ **TUNE IN** ►
to Tea Time with Team Epic Reads

   Find us at **www.epicreads.com**
and **@epicreads**